By
Alex Haley

The Autobiography of Malcolm X
Roots
A Different Kind of Christmas

A
DIFFERENT KIND
OF CHRISTMAS

ALEX HALEY

A DIFFERENT KIND OF CHRISTMAS

Doubleday

New York London Toronto Sydney Auckland

All of the characters in this book are fictitious, and any resemblance to actual persons, living or dead, is purely coincidental.

Published by Doubleday, a division of Bantam Doubleday Dell Publishing Group, Inc., 666 Fifth Avenue, New York, New York 10103

Doubleday and the portrayal of an anchor with a dolphin are trademarks of Doubleday, a division of Bantam Doubleday Dell Publishing Group, Inc.

BOOK DESIGN BY CAROL MALCOLM

To the memory of all those whose courage, daring, and self-sacrifice made the Underground Railroad possible.

A DIFFERENT KIND OF CHRISTMAS

*O*NE AFTERNOON in March of 1855, in his college office, whose austerity reflected his own lack of pretense and an honesty bordering at times on the severe, C. Thomas Ridgeley, the Dean of Men, considered the request of the stocky auburn-haired sophomore who stood formally at attention, as was required of a student appearing before an officer of the college. Fletcher Randall, a nineteen-year-old who had come north to Princeton, New Jersey, from North Carolina, had applied for permission to move to another dormitory. Dean Ridgeley glanced up from Randall's letter atop the student file which lay opened in the center of his otherwise bare desk.

"I see that you're requesting a transfer to another dormitory—rather late in the year, if I may say so—for 'personal reasons.' Would you care to elaborate on this?"

"It's a private matter, sir," Randall said.

"Let me remind you that as Dean of Men I tend to be concerned with the personal, sometimes even the private problems of the students. Now, may I hear more from you?"

"I believe you would understand, sir, that being a Southerner at the College of New Jersey is often a difficult proposition,"

Fletcher said. "And in my present dormitory, I keep running into problems with a Tom Barrett, a junior from New York. He and four or five of his cronies enjoy boasting that they're 'Rebel-haters.' I don't want to sound as if I've come here to whine to you, sir. I just feel I have to find other living quarters before something really unfortunate happens."

Dean Ridgeley chose to ignore the volatile sectional prejudices that had provoked this student conflict. He did not think this was the occasion to lecture on the snares and delusions of Southern chauvinism and its social repercussions, or the inhumanity of slavery (although he was tempted to quote Wordsworth's "Have I not reason to lament what man has made of man?"). After all, this young man was the product of a society and a caste which compared itself to the slaveholding civilizations of Greece and Rome. Fletcher Randall obviously was introspective by nature, not one of those Southern bloods who loved to ride and hunt and drink, not one given to the coarse jocosity so much a part of normal collegiate give-and-take.

Dean Ridgeley approximated a smile as he plucked from his top drawer a narrow, buff-colored envelope on which was tied a key. "Another dormitory has been approved, Mr. Randall. And you'll have a private room as usual. Your parents made it quite clear from the start that they wish to pay the extra fee because they felt a roommate would distract you from your studies. So, here is your new key, with my note of admission."

He looked at Fletcher Randall carefully. "Let me leave you with a thought. It's admirable that you've proved yourself to be such a consistently outstanding student. I was just looking into your record here, and you've placed in the top ten percent since you arrived. But you may be concentrating on scholarship to the exclusion of other important things, such as developing friendships." The dean again gave Randall the near-smile. "And Mr. Randall, try to remember for the future that changing neighborhoods is not always a solution to problems."

Pointedly, Dean Ridgeley glanced toward the doorway. "You are excused."

"Thank you, sir."

Fletcher Randall strode back to his current dormitory, greatly relieved that the dean had sanctioned his moving. Randall had indeed had his fill of the arrogant, hateful Tom Barrett, champion swimmer, Beau Brummel, and braggart, who missed no chance to mention that his father was a wealthy New York banker. And Barrett's cronies—Peter Estabrook, another swimmer, and Edgar Ascot of the famous men's clothing family, and Williams Gaines, whose father was a prominent lawyer. They all delighted in mocking and harassing Southern students, most especially Fletcher Randall, the solitary scholar, whose room was close to theirs in the dormitory. They loved to mimic Southern accents, to daub their faces with burnt cork in "yassuh, massa" caricatures of black slaves, or suddenly to bend nearly double and waddle forward, pretending they were cotton pickers.

Fletcher Randall's first collegiate summer at home had given him two months in which to reflect on the experiences of his freshman year, and he had returned for his sophomore year devoutly determined to accomplish two things. First, he would stay in Princeton for the next three summers, going home only for Christmases, and thereby earn his degree in three years. When he announced this to his parents, his father, a wealthy planter and state senator, had given one of his best senatorial roars, "By God, you do us proud, son, you do us proud!" And his mother, predictably, had wept at first and then had gone about dabbing her handkerchief at her eyes the rest of the day.

Secondly, Fletcher vowed to seize every opportunity to lay on his heaviest Southern accent when involved in any confrontation with Yankees.

Not that Fletcher had an easy time relating to his fellow Southerners at the college. During his freshman year he had been appalled by the alcoholic vulgarity which prevailed at gatherings in the South House, the favorite gathering place for Southerners just off the edge of the campus. Fletcher never would forget the time that the redheaded Georgian called "Rusty" Weaver had drenched him with a nearly full pitcher of beer, laughing like a hyena and bellowing drunkenly to all within his hearing, "Here's to one of them damned young North Carolina Tarheels!"

And there was short, heavyset, bushy-haired and foulmouthed "Hoss" Rankin, from a small town in Kentucky, who had somehow sensed that Fletcher was avoiding him, and reacted by seizing him from behind in his powerful wrestler's grip until Fletcher half-expected to hear his own ribs crack.

But the most annoying of the Southern contingent were those who heckled and made raw cracks and ribald jokes because his high grade averages were published each semester on the Dean's List, and because he lived alone, while most of them had roommates and enjoyed raucous visiting more than studying.

One night, for instance, Fletcher had come into South House bringing several books, as usual, and two class notebooks. He set them down and went for a cup of tea. When he returned, his books had disappeared. He hunted for them quietly at first, knowing it was someone's twisted idea of humor, but after half an hour he grew angry. And then the snickering began. He was on the verge of exploding at them all when a big bear of a junior classman, called appropriately "Ox" Baird, a Virginian, roared up and banged the top of a nearby table. "All right, goddammit, enough is enough! Give the Tarheel his books and let him get the hell out of here and go study, like a whole hell of a lot more of us ought to be doing instead of sitting here swilling this damn beer!" Somebody else had hollered drunkenly, "Fletcher, the pride of the South!" and someone else had led a drunken cheer as he left the South House in a welter of emotions.

It took less than an hour for Fletcher Randall to pack up and move his belongings across the campus and into his new room, where he soon was comfortably ensconced. That night Fletcher tackled his assignment for the next day, a composition for his English class on a current event of his choice. He had thought about writing an essay on the Silver Gray and Conscience Whigs, Northern members of the Whig party. The Conscience Whigs, mostly New Englanders, strongly opposed slavery. Whereas those who were willing to cooperate with Southern "cotton" Whigs were known as Silver Grays. But Fletcher finally decided he would try some sharply critical commentary on how in England, Mrs. H. B. Stowe, the author of *Uncle Tom's Cabin*, a book hated violently by all Southerners, was being received and honored by many of Great Britain's highest nobility and statesmen.

He was deeply engrossed in drafting the fourth page of his satire when at ten-thirty a soft knocking came at the door.

Who on earth? he thought. At this hour?

He opened the door and there stood three students who appeared to be almost the same age and bore a distinct resemblance to one another. The older one in the middle spoke: "We heard you moved here. We came to meet you. We are Friends."

Fletcher Randall felt six eyes focused on him, he heard the words, he sensed a special quality in these three young men. Their very calm was somehow forceful.

But Fletcher knew that he had to finish his assignment before he slept. "Glad to meet you, my name's Fletcher Randall," he heard himself say. "But I have to ask you to understand that I'm trying to write an assignment for a class tomorrow."

Appraised by the six eyes, he felt irritated.

The youngest of the three smiled. "I know, I'm in your English class."

Fletcher managed to smile back. "I thought so. So, look, can you all come back some better time?"

As the three nodded, he couldn't resist asking, "Aren't you all kin to each other?"

"Brothers," the middle one said. "We're from Philadelphia. Also we call ourselves Friends. You may have heard of our religion—we're Quakers. We wish to discuss with you a subject on which our views differ with yours."

The three turned and walked off down the hallway as quietly as they had come.

Fletcher went back to his composition. He was distracted every now or then when the word "Quakers" crossed his mind, and he strained to recall bits and pieces about that sect.

A religious group, yes. And an extremely pacifist people. He had heard that quality humorously illustrated by a joke: Late one night in a Quaker's home, a robber busily gathering up loot suddenly saw the Quaker standing in longjohns, pointing a shotgun, saying, "Friend, thee art standing where I am about to shoot."

Then it finally hit Fletcher Randall, and he wondered why he hadn't remembered this first of all: it was the Quakers whom his father deplored for their strong views against slavery, especially the keeping and selling of slaves.

He made up his mind that if the Quaker brothers wanted to debate the issue of slavery with him, whose family owned many slaves, then he would simply ask them to leave.

Through the rest of that week, Fletcher would remember how the Quaker brothers' eyes had assessed him as he stood in his doorway, as if they were trying to reach some decision concerning him.

At the next session of Fletcher's English class he made certain that he arrived early, then languished at the rear door until he spotted and exchanged nods of hello with the younger Quaker brother in his class, whose seat was toward the rear—probably intentionally, Fletcher thought, so as not to attract any more notice than possible. He did not recall ever having heard that Quaker brother say a word in the class.

On a Thursday afternoon Fletcher found a note slipped underneath his door, informing him that on Friday afternoon the Quaker brothers would again come to visit.

He told himself that probably their younger brother knew he had no Friday afternoon classes.

In the meantime, his curiosity concerning Quakers had intensified. His own favorite sophomore courses were history, geography, and moral philosophy, principally, he supposed, because like his mother he seemed to have been born possessed of a great curiosity about different peoples, and sought out books about the ways in which they lived and conducted themselves within their different historical places. Indeed, back in the library of the plantation mansion was a shelf filled with such literature, collected originally by his mother, some before he was born, and few things gave her greater pleasure than his passion for these books.

In fact, Fletcher's small boyhood secret ambition was that one day when he was grown, he would be sure that an experienced, qualified overseer was left to run his huge plantation and its essential multitude of slaves, and he would go traveling—on the transatlantic ships and thence by horse, or boat, or cart, or on foot, wherever in the world he felt most drawn to visit.

Fletcher's intense desire to learn more of the world and its people never really diminished. It was certainly not that he didn't love his North Carolina, the Tarheel state, and particularly his Ashe County, as well as his entire proud Southland and its whole plantation way of life. Of course he did! As a matter of fact, he had reminded himself again that whenever he would get together for a talk with the Quakers, or "Friends" as they called themselves, at the very outset he would emphatically make it clear that nothing disrespectful was to be said, or even implied, about his Southland's traditional way of life, else that would be the end of the conversation. But he hoped that would not happen, as he knew he would be intrigued to learn something new about those Quaker people, in the same way he had always looked forward to someday learning more about Italians, or Germans, or the Scots, or Jews, or Greeks.

Fletcher had heard, in fact, that quite a representation of the white European ethnic groups was to be found among the student body. He had heard that there was even a students' International House, which sometimes held open house, and he had promised himself to attend the next one. To prepare for the impending visit by the brothers, Fletcher had already spent one evening in the college library reading about the Quakers.

He found that in 1688, German Quakers at Germantown, Pennsylvania, had made official protest "against the traffic in the bodies of men and the treatment of men as cattle." By 1772 the New England Friends were beginning to expel members for failing to free their slaves. In 1776, the annual meetings of Quakers in both Philadelphia and New York had made slaveholding an expulsion offense. The Quakers, he learned, surpassed all other denominations in their general acceptance and advocacy of antislavery doctrine. In fact, Fletcher read, many Southern Quakers had moved to the North because of their hatred of slavery, and they had established important Underground Railroad work centers, especially in Ohio and Indiana. He read also that there were many Underground Railroad centers in southeastern Pennsylvania and in eastern Indiana because so many Quakers lived there.

Fletcher wondered how his mother would react to his actually meeting and talking with Quakers. His father's response, however, was predictable: he would roar in his most theatrical senatorial rage at the very thought of any son and heir of his voluntarily occupying the same room with anyone who opposed the idea of Southern plantations being maintained by the sweat and blood of black slaves, and the more slaves, the better.

On Friday afternoon the three brothers came to visit. Upon entering his room, the two younger ones each lightly clasped his hand on either side, then their free hands were clasped by the oldest brother, who softly prayed "that all men might become as brothers."

He was truly touched at their neighborly welcome. Then a sudden thought struck him. Could the Dean of Men possibly have had something to do with this? He pushed that possibility into the back of his mind to think about later.

Even though this time Fletcher was far better prepared, he still could not help feeling there was something almost mystical about the brothers. They seemed to move as one, almost to think as one. They projected such peacefulness that he knew they must harbor an aversion to violence, either verbal or physical. At the same time, he sensed that if the three Quaker brothers were ever sufficiently challenged and felt they had no other choice, then not only would they resist, they would fight to their deaths.

It intrigued Fletcher that he sensed all of these things about his visitors as the brief prayer ended, before any of the three had said a word.

But he spoke first. He said he felt it only honest to say he was pleased to have the chance to meet and talk with them, to learn something more of their people, of whom he had heard only bits and pieces in North Carolina where he had grown up. He had it at the tip of his tongue to warn them against criticizing his native South, but he refrained.

The younger brother, the one who was in Fletcher's English class, first introduced himself, then indicated the others. "I am Andrew Ellis, and my older brothers here are Paul and Noah."

As Fletcher shook their hands, his classmate said that even during the past year when he and Fletcher were freshmen, he had remarked to his brothers and to their family in Philadelphia of the Southerner's outstanding scholarliness, for which he said the Quaker people and their families felt the greatest respect.

The middle brother said they were from Philadelphia and they were proud that the Quaker people had much to do with that city's being called "The City of Brotherly Love."

And the oldest Quaker brother quietly added, "No religious group in the country equals the Quakers in standing up for the basics of human freedom, and equality, and dignity."

Fletcher could tell where the conversation was headed, and he made a decision to speak his mind on the provocative subject in as nonchallenging a manner as possible. He said he had read and heard that Quaker people were opposed to owning and working black slaves. "So I hope you can understand why I disagree with you. My daddy, and then his daddy before him, have owned and run what's said to be North Carolina's fourth-biggest plantation." Fletcher paused. "We have over a hundred slaves and three thousand acres, which probably one day I will inherit."

For a moment there was utter silence as the Quaker brothers seemed to consider that pronouncement. Then the oldest said, "People are different, and opinions by their nature cannot all be the same." Fletcher breathed a quiet sigh of relief. Apparently the Quakers were not going to make any overt attack against his family's slaveholding.

At the same time, Fletcher had a sense, from all of the things he had read and heard, that the Quakers, being Quakers, were

11

only biding their time, and that by no means was this going to be the end of it.

But to Fletcher's surprise, the next hour passed with no confrontational issues raised while the four of them sat either on his bed or on the two straight chairs his room contained. When he asked, the brothers told him more about themselves and about their family. They had been born a year apart. The oldest brother said he'd made up his mind to graduate in business, then join their father in running the family's large grocery and fruit produce business in Philadelphia. The younger two said they might also join the family business, but they had not yet fully decided.

Listening to them, Fletcher appreciated having followed his own instincts to meet some people he knew his father would have hated sight unseen, and surely would have warned him against. He realized he was experiencing some of the personal growth that came from broadening one's experiences, a process which the professor of his Tuesday morning moral philosophy class, Dr. C. Erick Lincoln, recommended from time to time.

And Fletcher enjoyed a further, privately amusing reflection: What would the Dean of Men think of him sitting there, talking so pleasantly, quietly, and calmly with his new Quaker friends?

The Quaker brothers—Fletcher found it perplexing that he did not think of them by their family surname as the Ellis brothers, but rather as the Quaker brothers—were preparing to leave when, upon what seemed to be totally an impulse, the older one turned about and said, "Friend Fletcher, you are so distant from your North Carolina, and our home in Philadelphia is so close. Since on Friday afternoons you do not have classes, why not be our guest next Friday when we are planning our weekend at home? We enjoy your company. You have not visited our Philadelphia, and our family would join us in being pleased to have you."

"I'd love to! I'd enjoy that!" Fletcher blurted out, he was that touched and taken aback.

The more he thought about it, the more exhilarated he felt. In his nineteen years, this was the first time he'd decided on his own to undertake such an adventure!

The brother had not spoken about any traveling specifics. Fletcher knew that now for some years, the Philadelphia and Reading Railroad had maintained a regular line to Philadelphia. But he told himself he would bet every cent he had that as Quakers to their bones, the brothers would not catch any new, modern, steam-belching train, but would travel their familiar round trip either by a commercial carriage or a rented one. He had once heard someone say that by carriage, stopping but once for a change of horses, it was about ten hours from Princeton to Philadelphia.

Nor had the brothers mentioned where he would stay during his weekend invitation. But he felt certain he would be a guest at their home.

He had a quick, unpleasantly embarrassing thought that he could not, impulsively or otherwise, invite the brothers into his own home.

He was glad that his mother had insisted he buy his new blue serge suit with the cambric shirt and string tie to match for formal occasions. But then he had a second thought: Yes, carry the suit, but something simpler might better fit the Quakers' plain way of life.

What would the "Quaker Friends" eat at home? Fletcher wondered. Likely they would never have heard of yellow hominy grits and red-eye gravy. But he remembered having read that numerous Quakers were farmers, some of them owners of major Southern plantations, which they physically worked either themselves or with paid day labor, refusing to use any slaves. He had read in pamphlets and periodicals in the college library that as early as the late 1600s, Quakers had established important centers of what came to be called the Underground Railroad, which helped Southern plantation slaves escape into the North, into Canada especially.

Reading that had so infuriated him that he had slapped the book down against the library table. Fletcher thought it approached treason for white men to help rob other white men of their black property, especially since slaves could be so expensive, and now even able-bodied women and children had begun costing almost as much as average slave black men.

Fletcher's curiosity worked overtime as the passing days brought him closer to the Friday of his eagerly awaited visit. For some reason, he thought it best that he not write his parents of his adventure until after it had happened.

II

*F*LETCHER HAD WORKED HIMSELF into a dither of anticipation by that Friday noon when the youngest Quaker brother arrived at the already opened door and said, smiling, "Our carriage is outside if you're ready."

They had rented a carriage, as he had guessed, a four-place surrey with an oiled fabric rainproof top, and the surrey was pulled by a fine, stout team of two. In the driver's seat was the oldest brother, Noah. The fabric roof was rolled back, for the weather was beautiful.

As the surrey rolled on through the scenic town of Princeton, Noah told Fletcher their traveling plans. They would ride at a comfortable rate for the next five to six hours, until about sundown, when they would stop for dinner and stay overnight at a favorite inn. Saturday morning they would rise early for a shorter ride and enter the city when its sights could best be appreciated.

"Even we who were born and reared there find that we're always anxious to get back," said Fletcher's classmate.

At least fifty questions were flashing through Fletcher's mind, but he instead took his companions' cue and silently enjoyed the passing roadside views. Automatically he found himself comparing the Ashe County, North Carolina, countryside with similar scenes he now observed as the surrey rode along over the next several hours through New Jersey and into Pennsylvania. It struck Fletcher how, in fact, everywhere that anyone went God's nature was evident, manifest in the plants, the animals, the earth, the rocks. He thought: All men are His creation in cities, and towns, and rural places.

It was nearing sundown when Noah pulled the team over, and they stopped before a two-storied inn. It had guest rooms on top, Fletcher could tell by the windows and curtains. He also caught a glimpse of about six additional small single-room cabins at the rear.

They all clambered out, and there appeared a very black old man with sparsely tufted, graying hair. He spoke briefly with Noah, and took the horses' reins to guide them to the stalls where they'd be fed and bedded down for the night.

Inside, the innkeeper and his wife were delighted to see the three brothers, and beamed their welcome at Fletcher and pumped his hand when he was introduced.

They were assigned rooms where they could wash up before they ate, and Fletcher was glad to be sharing one with his classmate. Privately he thought that he would really enjoy that companionship back at the college dormitory.

The dinner, eaten after Noah had said grace, was served by the couple assisted by their plump, equally congenial daughter. Fletcher felt it had to be his finest meal since he'd last sat at the great table in his family's mansion, eating the delicacies prepared by their incomparable old slave cook Hattie, with Mandy as her assistant. Old Black Hattie had been their family's housemaid and his nursemaid, and then, when he was a little boy, the cook. She had raised his father before him; and when each had been infants, Black Hattie had suckled them. She liked to tell people that God had given Fletcher his father's hotheadedness and stubbornness—and his mother's heart. Fletcher inwardly smiled at his memories of how usually Old Black Hattie would make-believe that she was furtively glancing about, lest she get caught, before slipping to him some tasty spoonfuls of samplings directly from her black iron cookpots. He remembered how he would blow furiously upon each spoonful to cool it enough to taste. And the tasting had always helped him to know which dishes to concentrate upon when the steaming platters were served in the dining room of the mansion, which by tradition the slaves always preferred to call the Big House.

Even back home, he had rarely stuffed himself as he did there at the inn's long table, and certainly never with any more relish. The boiled beef, roast pork, and chicken with dumplings were each spectacular, as were the seven choices of vegetables, and the peach cobbler.

Afterward, actually embarrassed, Fletcher excused himself and climbed upstairs and into his narrow bed, and he was soundly snoring when his roommate shortly followed.

He ate much less breakfast, although the food was plentiful and varied. When they were ready to leave and the innkeeper's bill was to be paid, his share came to $2.20 for the food and lodging, and then, outside, another fifty cents toward the old black man's care of the horses, which he had freshly curried and brushed until their coats were shining. In a sudden impulsive burst of expansiveness, Fletcher flipped another ten-cent piece in a high arc, which the old black man deftly caught, simultaneously grinning and bowing gratefully, "Yessuh, thanky, suh, yessuh, sho' do!"

The clear, bright Saturday morning enhanced the rest of the scenic way as the carriage continued toward the city of Philadelphia.

Even on the outskirts, Fletcher began to realize that however much he had read of this major city, he was not prepared for its impact now that it actually was a physical fact before his eyes. As the horses' rhythmic clopping kept the wheels of the carriage rolling along smoothly, he was awed at the sight of so many houses, obviously with so many people living so much more closely together than ever would be dreamed of within the plantation region of Ashe County, North Carolina. Sitting up there on the carriage seat, Fletcher made a flash vow that whatever his future might bring, it was absolutely going to include finding a way also to visit the legendary city of New York, as well as Boston and other cities, especially those that had played crucial historical roles in the early United States. He was also determined to visit the southern city of Norfolk, Virginia, famed for its waterfront, which he had read was as large as, although less busy than, the waterfront of Philadelphia.

Fletcher stared at the people walking in every direction. Glimpses of many of their faces, and sometimes of their clothing, told him they were from different countries; he wished he could ask each one where he was from.

But what was shocking were the numbers and especially the cocky strutting and mannerisms of black people! Fletcher had read that Philadelphia contained mostly free black people, and actually seeing them was an experience he was going to have to think about later. Growing more clearly visible, although yet at some distance, were many buildings which Fletcher could see were huge beyond belief. "As we get farther into the business areas, we'd like you to meet some of our friends," Noah said, holding the reins loosely, and Fletcher nodded with enthusiasm.

He imagined that he would be meeting other Quakers, or "Friends," much the same as his hosts, but Noah's first stop was to greet "Mr. Destito," an Italian man in his fifties with a big "Fine Harness and Saddle" sign hung out on his storefront. The Italian fairly trotted around the carriage, wringing each brother's hands, exclaiming "Oh, *miei amici*! How are your family?" It turned out that he and the father of the Quaker brothers had first met as immigrants on the same ship from Europe which arrived in Philadelphia where they later found work together. Finally Mr. Ellis, the Quaker, had turned to selling vegetables on a pushcart, and Mr. Destito had chosen his native Italian love of leatherworking. They had both done well over the years, their families had stayed close, and the Destitos' only son was at Yale College.

The horses kept up their clopping pace along the cobblestoned streets, Noah stopping them at intervals to introduce the fascinated Fletcher to a Dutch merchant of easily twenty-five or more kinds of cheeses, and a German butcher whose store window was festooned with more coils and links and varieties of sausages than all of the cattle- and hog-raisers in North Carolina would ever have dreamed existed.

Plodding along another street, Noah slowed the horses, and Fletcher sensed that his hosts had become less talkative, as if something here was going to be different. Then the carriage stopped before a large, wide building that bore an oblong block-printed sign, "Fortas—Sailmakers."

"I want you to meet one of Philadelphia's most successful men," said Noah, as he jumped down and quickly went inside the building. Fletcher tensed upon seeing a mixture of both white and black men moving in and out of the wide front entrance, all of them wearing the same white overalls, and all of them obviously working as equals together.

Noah returned, and walking beside him, talking and smiling, was a black man.

"Mr. Randall, meet Mr. Fortas, our family's friend, our city's finest sailmaker, and one of our most prosperous businessmen." Fletcher almost collapsed as if shot. He felt his face flush hot as the black man shook his hand. As if he were an equal! "A pleasure, sir," Fortas said. Fletcher could say nothing, and he knew that his three host brothers saw his face turn crimson. It was merciful when a thin, overalled black worker hastened up and said the owner was quickly needed inside.

The carriage pulled away. The Quaker brothers sat like apostrophes. Fletcher's right hand felt indelibly soiled. Involuntarily, he shoved the hand deeply into his right pants pocket. He knew that the brothers had seen him do that, too. He was experiencing such mixed embarrassment and fury that he even thought of springing from the carriage down onto the cobblestoned street to find his own way back to the college—and perhaps just pick up his clothes and books and keep on to Ashe County, North Carolina, where no such affrontery would be remotely possible.

The six Quaker eyes were upon his every move now, and he did not care. They knew he had been born on a Southern slave plantation, and reared there; they should understand his reaction to that presumptuous darky. It was one thing to embrace the house darkies. But to endure familiarity from a black stranger was intolerable! Fletcher just hoped they didn't plan to introduce him to anyone else; he wouldn't care if it were the Governor of Pennsylvania.

But from the moment the carriage entered the driveway of the Ellis family's large, attractive home, Fletcher, furious though he was, had to succumb to the utter graciousness of the father and mother, as well as that of the lovely pig-tailed daughter, Emilie, eleven years old.

They were all clearly joyous that their family was together again, and that the brothers' Southern friend had been brought as an unexpected guest. Mrs. Edith Ellis, in fact, actually resembled Fletcher's mother, both in physique and mannerisms, and he boldly told her so. Impulsively hugging him, Mrs. Ellis explained, "And I adopt thee, Fletcher, here now as my newest son."

The father, Mr. Eugene Ellis, was no less genial and genteel. After showing Fletcher to his room, to bathe quickly and change clothes, Mr. Ellis said, "The boys and I would like to drive you around this afternoon to let you enjoy our city. We want you to like it so much you will want to come back."

"I'd love to! Yessir!"

In the Ellises' six-passenger family landau, again the eldest son was driving, with Fletcher as the front-seat passenger beside him, the better to see clearly everything that the father, Mr. Ellis, explained from just behind Fletcher on the second seat.

As an awesome start, they all got out of the carriage at Independence Hall. Fletcher gazed open-mouthed at the historic gray stone structure within which the Framers had struggled for months, hammering out the Constitution of the United States. And right there before his eyes hung the famed Liberty Bell, which had pealed out its messages of freedom and democracy! Fletcher stared at the bell's historic crack.

Everywhere he saw and heard vendors loudly crying or barking out their amazing range and variety of wares to sell. He repeatedly exclaimed his amazement at seeing so many clearly different nationalities. "The city's immigrant population is steadily swelling nowadays, especially with Germans and Huguenots," the father said.

Fletcher deliberately made no comment about the scores of blacks he saw walking about confidently, with their heads high, as if they considered themselves as good as whites. He thought how Southern plantation blacks were taught from infancy, above everything else, to stay in their place—or else.

It was as if Mr. Ellis had read Fletcher's mind. "We all understand that it's much different down in the South where you live," he said. "Slavery was outlawed here in Philadelphia in 1770, so most blacks you see are free, although still too many are slaves, more's the pity. But like our sailmaker Mr. Fortas, quite a few are prospering—as carpenters and plasterers and bricklayers and house painters and especially caterers. In fact, Philadelphia's busiest caterer is Thomas Dorsey, who was a slave who came here on the Underground Railroad." Mr. Ellis paused. "One reason our city appreciates black people is that during our yellow fever epidemic, most black people didn't flee; they stayed within the city and nursed the terribly sick."

Fletcher made no comment. He thought that, whatever, he must not again embarrass himself; he simply had to respect the sincerity and forthrightness of these Quaker people. Mr. Ellis changed the subject.

"Would you like to see the waterfront where the ships come in?"

"I sure would!" exclaimed Fletcher.

The landau rolled along. Half an hour later, Fletcher could scarcely believe he was witnessing such a spectacle of docks and piers and all the different kinds and sizes of sailing ships, either moored at their piers or anchored out in the harbor so thickly that their masts, silhouetted against the sky, were like a forest in the wintertime.

"I wanted so much for you to see one of the great immigrant ships unloading their passengers. That's a sight never to forget," Mr. Ellis said. "But we appear to have arrived at the wrong time." There was scarcely any activity to be seen on the several large immigrant ships, obviously soon to return to Europe. A babble of different languages came from sailors milling about or standing in knots talking or filtering in and out of the scores of waterfront business enterprises, ranging from the huge ship chandlers to the sleaziest small dives and taverns with scantily clad women occasionally parading their obvious wares outside.

Leaving the waterfront, Noah guided the carriage at a prudent distance alongside one of the city's new steam-powered streetcars. "They handle as well as the horsecars, and as you can see, they move faster," said Mr. Ellis. He added that not too long ago Pennsylvania was discovered to be a source of a new fuel called petroleum, a light and cleanly combustible fuel that was wonderful for things such as cookstoves.

They were clopping right along when Noah glanced sidewise

at Fletcher. "You don't expect to miss seeing our Quaker place of worship?"

Fletcher, smiling, shook his head. Within a little while they all got out of the carriage again and walked around before the famous Friends Meeting House.

In a little while, Mr. Ellis gently took Fletcher's arm and led him off a little way, obviously to speak privately. "I understand my sons are reluctant to ask you after your meeting Mr. Fortas, but will you now accompany us to an occasion we attend some Saturdays? I tell you in advance you will witness both races working for a common cause, which might broaden your experience, even though you disagree. You have my word that you will be asked to meet no one."

Fletcher's very soul screamed *"No!"* Yet in some way Mr. Ellis's simple, direct Quaker honesty was like a quiet solemn force that made it impossible to refuse him. Against his will, Fletcher forced his head to nod. Again, he was embarrassed, as he was also angered that he had ever accepted the Ellis brothers' invitation to visit in the first place. He knew now that once back at the college, the Quaker brothers and he would have no further contact. In his anger he grasped at their father's pledge that he would not be asked to meet anyone else. He simply could not comprehend anybody thinking or speaking about black people as if they were the same as white people.

The carriage stopped, and Fletcher saw ahead of them a moderate crowd that seemed to average three white people to each black, all of them filtering and shifting about for better standing places before a small, brownish, covered tent. When they got out of the carriage a young, wiry, obviously European immigrant white boy led their team to where there were dozens more horses with their carts, buggies, and carriages behind the hitching racks. As they walked closer, for an instant Fletcher closed his eyes. He had just glimpsed, sitting in folding chairs on the tent stage, two white and two black men wearing dark suits, white shirts, and ties.

Rising abruptly, one of the white men began loudly exhorting the crowd: "More will have to be done to help our black brothers and sisters, whom some call *slaves*, escape to freedom!"

Fletcher felt as he once had, years before, when he slipped off with some classmates from the academy and visited a tent in which some backwoods religious sect had prayed as they handled live rattlesnakes. He stood disbelieving the crowd's applause. Next, a black speaker rose and beckoned toward the audience. Within a moment, climbing the steps while glancing warily over both shoulders was an extremely ragged, barefoot, short, powerfully built black man holding a burlap sack behind his neck to cover his shoulders.

"Maceo here escaped. He hid by day and ran following the North Star at night, despite his overseer and slave hunters with guns and bloodhounds. He just reached safety here night before last, and has been sleeping almost every minute since!"

Amidst the crowd's applause the black speaker paused dramatically. "You think Maceo looks all right to you? Well, just take a look at Maceo's back!"

He pulled the burlap sack off the black man's shoulders, revealing a mess of welts, some partly healed, others still infected. Amid the horrified sounds of the crowd, many of whom were in tears, the speaker yelled, "Now all hold up your hands who would vote to send Maceo back to slavery!"

"No, no, no!" shouted the crowd. "Well then," cried the

speaker, "let's dig deep in our pockets to help the three million more slaves in the South who cannot escape—unless we help!"

The crowd was pressing forward, dropping bills and coins into the black speaker's can, when the second white speaker rose, yelling like a country revival preacher.

"Think of our enslaved black brothers and sisters—tired and weary of chopping down forests to clear new acres to farm for their master! Think of dragging and filling twelve-foot-long cotton-picking sacks that get as heavy as rocks! Think of working your hardest and being beaten and lashed to try and make you work yet harder—to keep your cruel masters and their spoiled families fat and rich! Think of those who have now decided they must *escape* all this! They must *escape* the cotton fields and the rice swamps! Black men and women and their children, and those without any family, their families dead from the perils of slavery, often from being beaten, or worked to death! All over the South, and in the border slave states, they are waiting for the signal to escape! They are waiting to see an Underground Railroad conductor nod, or hear him whisper a snatch of the right song, or hear the hoot owl's call, or any other signal telling them, 'All right, brother or sister, the time is *now*! Let's escape to the North!' And they're out there at night, running and hiding in the caves and the thickets, and rowing for their lives in little skiffs with cruel men and dogs on the banks seeking big rewards for catching them and dragging them back in irons to be tortured until they scream, until they drop! Have *mercy* on them, oh God, and support our work!" The speaker gasped for more breath, and he found it to use in a last appeal, "Let us *all* follow the North Star to the freedom of our souls, which can not be free so long as our brethren are in chains!"

Fletcher wanted to shout out to the crowd that to his knowledge no such cruelties had ever been inflicted on those black slaves on his family's plantation. He stood feeling as if he'd just been scalded. He wanted to scream to them that his father, his mother, and he himself treated their treasured house slaves practically as members of their family. The slaves knew their place; that was the main difference. He could not truly say what happened to some of the field slaves at the hands of the overseers, because in fact he had heard of some beatings given to discipline a wayward slave or to punish captured runaways. In fact, the only time he'd ever known his mother to scream at his father was the day an overseer who had just caught a runaway came proudly to their mansion's back porch with blood on his coat. "Get that creature away from this house!" his mother had screamed.

The revival shouter called another recently escaped slave to the stage. He silently removed his shirt and turned to reveal his back, whose granulation ridges bespoke a history of many beatings; it resembled a washboard.

The Ellis father and sons had been observing Fletcher's face. No one spoke as the father began leading them back toward the carriage.

Fletcher felt that as a Southerner who had trusted quiet, peaceful-acting Quakers, he had been exploited. Back at the Quakers' home, forcing himself to be civil, he managed to get through most of the dinner before politely excusing himself, hastening to his room, and vomiting up whatever he had eaten.

Fletcher Randall, heir-apparent to his powerful state senator father's vast three-thousand-acre cotton, tobacco, and livestock plantation, worked by over one hundred slaves, vowed that after bidding goodbye to the Ellis family in Philadelphia, he would utter not a single word during the long Sunday nonstop carriage ride from the City of Brotherly Love back to the college. He reasoned that their invitation had invited his trust, which had been atrociously breached.

Within the first hour of traveling Fletcher pointedly established his grim silence as deliberate, and Noah commenced with his brothers a quiet conversation about Quaker topics entirely alien to the fourth passenger.

Upon their arrival that night at the college, the Ellises' good nights at the dormitory were as terse as Fletcher's mumbled response. And then, once inside his room, he threw down his bag and flung himself across his bed, weeping tears of rage and beating the mattress with his fists.

Fletcher decided not to write his regular Sunday-night letter to his mother and father. On the one hand, he did not wish to say that he had visited the major city of Philadelphia and then not share at least the highlights of his experiences there. But he was never going to admit to such wanton carelessness as having actually shaken a nigger's hand, and he was certainly not going to report that he had stood on the fringes of an Underground Railroad crowd celebrating the escape of Southern plantation slaves. Fletcher decided that he would write home later during the week.

The soft knocking sounded against his door the following afternoon. Standing before his closet, pulling on his light sweater, he was getting ready to go out to eat at the students' cafeteria, then visit the college library for some research. He stood very still, and the knocking came again. He imagined that he heard footsteps going away.

Fletcher passed up going to dinner; he ate instead from a box that his mother had sent of Old Black Hattie's homemade cookies and other treats, and soon grew nauseated. He felt strangely agitated. Exactly what was going on in Fletcher's head he could not identify. It seemed to be roiling about on its own, and at times he wondered if the whip-scarred black backs, the words of the preacher-like speakers, might not have left some kind of psychic laceration within him.

He wished there were someone whom he could trust enough to talk with, to ask his opinion of the whole matter, and if possible his advice. He had never before given any really serious thought to darkies. They had always simply been there, a part of the plantation property, not really too unlike the livestock. Those who worked out in the field the overseer presided over, using his own methods, and it was not expected that the master or his family would know the names of any of those field slaves, only those who served and cared for the family directly in the big house, such as Old Black Hattie, or Mandy, or Moses. But not even those felt they deserved any special concern.

He wished that he had not witnessed the Underground Railroad rally, for he knew he was not going to forget it. And he knew that he would feel its significance in ways he could not even begin to define.

Fletcher thought maybe there was one person to whom he might unburden himself, one who he knew would be startled if asked, but who probably would give him some listening time, and that would be his professor Dr. C. Erick Lincoln, who taught the moral philosophy class. But he couldn't summon up the nerve to approach him.

By the week's end, Fletcher was miserable. In his English class, he arrived very early and hastened to his assigned seat near the front. He kept his eyes straight ahead until the class was dis-

missed. He still sat for a little while, engrossed in writing something, until he seemed no longer to feel upon him the Quaker classmate's eyes from five rows behind. Then Fletcher also left.

In the quiet and privacy of the college library, to which he seemed to be drawn over the next several weeks, Fletcher searched after some answers for himself.

At the card files, he was able to locate the subject headings he wanted. Then he carefully spaced his book or pamphlet requests in a manner consistent with a student's essay research, so that they wouldn't arouse the curiosity of any of the librarians. He requested sources about the Underground Railroad and the Philadelphia Vigilance Committee, and books and pamphlets and reports about both the free and the enslaved blacks.

He read bent over the materials on his library desk, so that anyone passing close to him would not be likely to identify the subject matter. He'd had no idea that the Underground Railroad had acquired its name around 1831 when an escaping Kentucky slave named Tice Davids jumped into the Ohio River barely ahead of his master and hired slave catchers, who grabbed a boat and rowed their hardest after him, watching him steadily as he swam. He thrashed ashore on the Ohio side, and suddenly dashed from the sight of his baffled and angrily cussing Kentucky pursuers, who could find no trace of him. One exclaimed, "He must've gone off an underground road!" As the story got told over and over, when steam trains were exciting the North, the quote became "underground railroad," and those who helped slave fugitives came to be called "conductors," and "station-masters," or "brakemen," or "firemen."

The Underground Railroad and the Vigilance Committee, though almost synonymous in their goal of helping the enslaved blacks find freedom, were individually quite different, Fletcher discovered.

The growth of the Underground Railroad had led to the founding of extremely supportive Vigilance Committees, composed of both blacks and whites, in cities such as New York, Boston, and Philadelphia. Philadelphia's Vigilance Committee, the strongest of all, had been founded in 1838 by a free black man named Robert Purvis. The Vigilance Committees gave fugitive slaves clothes, food, legal protection, and subsistence funds to help them either settle down or continue toward their destination. The destination most often was Canada. But Illinois, Indiana, and Ohio also had outstanding reputations for anti-slavery activities, and for receiving and assisting the greatest number of fugitives, most of whom came up the Mississippi or across the Ohio River.

With an obsessed intensity, Fletcher studied the laws concerning the slave trade. A law passed by Congress in 1807 prohibiting the slave trade wound up making slave smuggling profitable, because Southern planters desperately needed more slaves for their cotton plantations, a vastly bigger business since the 1793 invention of the cotton gin.

As the Northern states made slavery illegal, more and more Southern slaves began trying to escape into the North in search of freedom.

The gradually expanding and improving escape network saw the runaways generally move in the dark of night, frequently led by the Quakers. They and other friends of the fugitives would hide them during the day, and at night escort them to the next safe road or trail or stream. It was a dangerous business, with the fugitives advertised and described in the newspapers, and steadily sought by slavecatchers with their bloodhounds and search warrants and guns.

31

The Underground Railroad agents had to take the boldest of chances, and they risked and sometimes actually lost their own lives when it was they who got captured. And, Fletcher read, of all Underground Railroad activity, the greatest was in Philadelphia.

Finally, in 1850, the Fugitive Slave Law was passed, fining or imprisoning whoever was convicted of helping a slave escape. The Underground Railroad responded with even greater activity than before, with the Quakers in the forefront. Some former slaves risked their lives repeatedly, returning to rescue their families and others left behind. The Maryland black escapee Harriet Tubman returned so often, bringing out so many fugitives, that infuriated white slaveholders pooled an eventual forty thousand dollars as a reward for her capture.

But without white people the Underground Railroad, or UGRR, could not have worked. Fletcher read that some agents went South in their professional capacities as teachers or ministers, for example, using their positions to assist the anti-slavery cause. Others collected information about plantations, their owners, the numbers of slaves and overseers, to feed to the UGRR for its files. Some of these white people were caught, imprisoned, flogged, hanged, or even tortured to death.

Each night after leaving the library, Fletcher would take the longest route back to his dormitory, walking slowly, his mind wrestling with the fact that he had never before known so much about black slaves—or cared to know.

III

*F*LETCHER'S MOTHER was exasperated and worried. Her letter said, "*What* is *wrong* with you? Your father and I are upset! *No* letter, not even a *card* from our *son* for *six weeks*! You cannot *imagine* the *terrible* things we have thought!"

Fletcher had also been guilty of another delinquency, to a degree which brought him a summons to report on a Friday afternoon to the office of the Dean of Men.

This time he found the dean's entire demeanor considerably changed. As before, he was standing as Fletcher entered, but now he gestured to the chair across from his desk. "Have a seat, Mr. Randall. It is evident that we badly need to talk."

"Yes, sir."

"Your grades have fallen abysmally. You were doing splendidly in our three-year graduation program, but your grade average now has reached the probationary level. This coming summer, arduous remedial work will be required to raise your average to acceptable. Do you realize that?"

"Yes, sir."

The practiced eyes searched Fletcher. Dean Ridgeley had experienced many kinds of college student dramas. He had unearthed problems resulting from the pressure of parental academic expectations and helped solve them. He had advised young men awash in romance, or those near hysteria and shock at having impregnated a lover. The dean had been an arbiter with professors who intimidated. And he had seen severe depressions lead to suicides in dormitory closets.

"You are an outstanding student, Mr. Randall, but lately something is amiss." The dean was careful to emphasize the present tense. "Mr. Randall, tell me what's wrong; let me try to be helpful."

Fletcher looked back at him levelly. "My last time here, sir, you said that changing neighborhoods wasn't always the answer to a problem, and you were right. My problem is inside me, and right now, I'm trying to find a way to live with myself."

By half the way through the summer session, a hard, disciplined regimen of study had rescued Fletcher's grade point average. Then, as he had pledged to himself, he allotted a full weekend to return to Philadelphia—this time alone.

On the way, Fletcher was somber and preoccupied, unable to savor his first experience of riding in one of the swaying modern coaches of the new Philadelphia and Reading Railroad. He hastened through the huge Philadelphia station, and outside to the lineup of hired buggy drivers. The first driver he queried knew of "Fortas—Sailmakers" and its address.

Fletcher rode along feeling a certain numbness of determination. And when the hired buggy finally slowed as it approached the wide building where the white-overalled black and white workers carried material back and forth, Fletcher leaned forward and told the driver that he wouldn't be long, please to wait.

A white worker went agreeably to tell Mr. Fortas there was a visitor. When Mr. Fortas appeared, Fletcher saw at a glance that he had only a vague recollection of their meeting. "You met me with the Ellis brothers from Princeton," he said.

"Oh, yes!" The recognition lighted up Mr. Fortas's face, and Fletcher hoped that he didn't remember the rest of what happened. But he said, "I've come back to see you because I need you to permit me to shake your hand."

The sailmaker looked puzzled. "I need to explain," Fletcher said, which he did candidly.

"I understand," Mr. Fortas said. "It wasn't an unusual experience for me." He reflected for a moment. "What is remarkable, and heartening, is that you came back."

"I haven't come back for your sake. I came back for mine," Fletcher said. He was careful not to say "mister" or "sir."

"I thank you. I'll not soon forget what you've done," replied Mr. Fortas. "May I ask if you'd care to see our factory? I'll be honored to have a worker show you through."

"No—I appreciate your offer, but I'll take up no more of your time, and I have my buggy waiting."

Mr. Fortas stepped back. "Of course. You are welcome to come here any time."

"Thank you," Fletcher said. He went back to the hired buggy and gave the driver the Ellis family's greengrocer's address.

He asked the driver to circle the block, and as they passed the greengrocer's store he saw that it was teeming with customers. Fletcher said to the driver, "Please stop here, and wait for me."

For a while he just stood on the sidewalk, with people bustling past. Finally, when he felt that he had sufficiently grappled with his shame and embarrassment, he mustered the courage to walk inside.

Amidst one cluster of bargaining women patrons, Fletcher and the eldest Ellis brother, Noah, saw each other at the same instant. Noah dropped a head of lettuce as he came rushing to Fletcher and seized him in an embrace.

"I'm glad to see you looking so well," Fletcher said.

"I'm serving as my family's manager here now, the way it was planned," Noah replied.

Before he'd left Princeton, Fletcher had rehearsed what he wanted to say a hundred times, then repeated it again on the train, and he now conveyed it in a manner as direct and honest as he knew the Quakers were:

"Can you and your brothers and family forgive me? I need that. If it isn't too much to ask—"

"You don't have to ask," Noah said warmly. Then he added, "My father and brothers just went home to have their lunch. Andrew and Paul are here for the summer. They'll be happy to see you. Can you stay awhile?"

"No, that must be another time," Fletcher said. "And I'll look forward to it. But I have some personal business to attend to now."

"My family will understand, as I do," Noah replied. "At first—yes, we knew anger; we are human beings. But then, later on, we decided that through us you were experiencing great personal strain, and we prayed you would one day return, as

you now do. I believe you know that we Friends are great be-
lievers in prayer."

"I thank you, my friend."

Fletcher turned and went back to the hired buggy.

"Where to now, sir?" the driver asked.

"To Independence Hall."

He wanted to look again at that historic gray stone edifice,
this time from his widened perception of human frailties. Because, as he had furthered his researches at the college library,
he had come to realize the monumental irony that when the
Framers had signed the new Constitution, with its ringing promise of freedom and justice for all mankind, many among them
—indeed, some of the most prominent ones—were slaveowners.

Although Fletcher had not come to Philadelphia intent on
repeating the trauma he'd experienced at the weekly Saturday
rally held by the Philadelphia Vigilance Committee and the Underground Railroad, he found himself asking the driver to take
him there.

"I won't be able to wait for you, sir," the man said tautly.

"That will be fine." Fletcher wished he felt a fraction as confident about what he was doing as he hoped he had made his
voice sound.

At the rally, he discovered his feelings of rage had returned.
He stood angrily, sullenly, hearing one after another of the
speakers, most of them black, tearing passionately at the crowd's
emotions, as more recently escaped slaves showed off their hid-
eously scarred backs. He was furious at those who had made it
possible to indict the South by wantonly inflicting the terrible
beatings—usually bestial overseers, according to the escapees,

or sometimes the plantation owners themselves. And several fugitive slave women described incredible physical cruelties done by their former mistresses.

Fletcher did not remain long. He hailed a buggy letting off a passenger and returned to the railroad station.

Back in his dormitory room, Fletcher seriously considered leaving college and returning home. His father would be at first disappointed and upset. Having a scholastically outstanding son outdoing most Yankee students at the prestigious College of New Jersey at Princeton was a jewel in his politically ambitious father's crown. But he also knew that his father, before too long, would not only understand but would start boasting afresh of how his son had proved himself a chip-off-the-old-block in coming back to assume responsibility. Of course his mother would weep—for weeks, probably. Still, she'd be glad at the same time to have him home for good. Yes, Fletcher thought, maybe he ought to go back home to stay, and begin learning how to be the master of the plantation. For in time to come he would inherit it all; he was the only child, and it was expected that he would do his utmost to carry on in the family tradition. He thought of ways he could try to improve the lot of his slaves. He would see to it that all old faithful slaves were treated well, as they richly deserved, for their lifelong hard work and loyalty and devotion.

On the following Tuesday morning Dr. Lincoln concluded his lecture about the instinctive drive within all human beings for positive identities, and for freedom within their societies.

Then he held up a sheet of paper filled with cursive writing. "Gentlemen, this is a copy I have obtained of a letter that was written recently, and I believe it makes the points more eloquently than my lecture."

He adjusted his eyeglasses and surveyed the class. "Now, I should like for each of you to take out your notebook and a pen and be prepared to copy this letter. I will read it carefully, allowing you plenty of time."

There was a rustling of twenty-eight notebooks being opened, and then total silence. Professor Lincoln began reading, slowly and distinctly:

" 'In a composite Nation like ours, made up of almost every variety of the human family . . . there should be as before the Law . . . no rich, no poor, no high, no low . . . no black, no white . . . but one country, one citizenship, equal rights . . . and a common destiny for all.

" 'A government that can not or does not protect . . . the humblest citizen in his right . . . to life, liberty and the pursuit of happiness . . . should be reformed or overthrown without delay.' "

After reading the last word, "delay," Professor Lincoln said, "Gentlemen, there this letter ends. Now, may I ask, can any of you here identify the author?"

The students glanced about at one another. No one knew the answer. Fletcher sat thinking the author sounded like one of the shapers of the Constitution, and he looked forward to reading that letter from his notebook more than once again, for sure, and probably memorizing it, as well as writing the next week's two thousand words of comment.

Professor Lincoln again held up the letter. "Gentlemen, it was written by a man who had been a slave, a black man born into bondage in the State of Maryland . . . but his master finally taught him to read and write . . . and then he managed to escape."

The entire class sat up straighter. "His name, gentlemen: the author of that letter is Frederick Douglass!" Professor Lincoln paused for effect. "How many of you have heard of Frederick Douglass?"

Five students raised their hands. Professor Lincoln said, "I have a good drawing of him which I will share with you."

Professor Lincoln held up a portrait done in ink, then handed it to the nearest student. "Gentlemen, we have just sufficient class time remaining for you to pass this along among you, quickly."

When the portrait reached Fletcher, he stared down hard and felt drawn by the image of the leonine black man whose fiery eyes burned within a face that seemed to have the craggy strength of granite.

For the next several weeks Fletcher mostly tossed and turned through the nights, and dreamed things that he could only remember as being eerie.

One night as that summer's academic session ended, Fletcher felt that finally he perceived what he had been seeking; it came to him as a simple, clear signal. He threw back the covers and went over to his desk, and in the same moral philosophy notebook into which he had copied the Frederick Douglass letter he wrote down his thought, as if it were a poem of sorts:

"When a human being is capable of writing this letter, if that human being is in bondage, in *slavery*—if that human being is another being's *property*—then the bondage, the slavery, is *wrong*."

IV

*O*N A RAINY September morning, the director of the Philadelphia Vigilance Committee, Northern Area, was in the midst of one of his periodic visits with the chief conductor of the Northern Area Underground Railroad. As the two men shared the same essential goal of helping Southern slave fugitives find freedom somewhere in the North, they tried to get together at least once each month, primarily to weigh what needs were best fulfilled by one or the other agency or, in some instances, by both agencies interacting closely together.

Their conversation was interrupted when a black former slave, training to become a clerk, knocked at the director's door and, given permission to enter, announced that standing and waiting in the drizzling rain outside was a young white man who said he was from a college and who insisted that he must see the director. The clerk said he had told the young man that no one was admitted to the building unless he knew the password— which was changed each week—but that after being rained upon for the past half hour the young man still refused to go away.

The Vigilance Committee director exchanged a puzzled look

with the Underground Railway chief conductor, who said, "I'm just as curious as you are."

"All right, bring him in," the Vigilance Committee director told the clerk.

Then he said to the conductor, "Three or four times every year, college youngsters get persistent, they even get aggressive, wanting an interview so they can write about specifics of our activities here. I mean they want the facts, and figures, and details. I usually try to tell them in a nice way that by the nature of our work, we can not cooperate."

"Published interviews that might help identify our secret station agents would wipe us out." The UGGR conductor pushed himself up from the chair. "Just for whatever time you'll need with this fellow, I'll step outside."

"Oh, no! You stay put right where you are! Nothing will present any risk to us, I guarantee that!"

At the knock, the director barked "Come in!"

The clerk had taken the young man's raincoat, but the unprotected lower legs of his pants were so dripping wet that as Fletcher entered, to the clerk's obvious distress water still drained onto the floor. The director gestured to the clerk to close the door.

For a few seconds, the two older men appraised the younger one. It was apparent that Fletcher had not expected to see anyone except Mr. McDonald, the Vigilance Committee director. He was plainly disconcerted.

The director gestured Fletcher to a chair. "We are impressed by your standing out there in the rain, but you have interrupted our meeting, so please be brief."

Employ the manner of the Quakers, Fletcher had carefully

rehearsed himself. *Speak calmly and honestly, and be direct.* Despite his tension, he somehow managed that. Simply and clearly, he stated to them who he was: a junior in college at Princeton, the third-generation scion of a powerful and wealthy North Carolina state senator who owned that state's fourth-largest plantation—which was tilled by more than one hundred slaves.

The two older men were keenly attentive.

"Why do you attend college in Princeton?"

"My father recognizes the quality of a Northern education, sir, and he considers us superior to most of the Yankees."

McDonald assumed his most serious expression. "What has brought you here today?"

"I want to volunteer, sir."

"Well, now! So you're a young slaveholder who's going to help us out!"

"Try to trust me, sir."

Even Fletcher realized how ridiculous he sounded. "At least, just hear me, sir—"

McDonald glanced at his clock. "You have five minutes." The director shifted his position within his chair and glanced at his colleague, who nodded.

Fighting back his jitters, Fletcher forced himself to control his voice. He described his stormy relationship with the Yankee students, and his incompatibility with his Southern classmates. He told of his and his parents' pride that his upper-third scholarship average had enabled him to gain acceptance into the three-year degree program of attending the summer sessions with only Christmas holidays at home.

Fletcher recounted his meeting the three Quaker brothers,

and the visit to Philadelphia. He told how he'd been introduced to a black sailmaker Friend, whose handshake had outraged him. He told how the Quaker brothers' father urged him to a joint rally of the Vigilance Committee and the Underground Railroad.

With his emotions as visible as if they were painted upon him, Fletcher did his best to describe how he was rocked and shaken to the core by the things he heard and saw.

The director and the UGRR conductor leaned slightly forward, rapt with the young man's transparent baring of his soul.

He anguished through an account of renouncing his Quaker friends, and related how something which seemed as powerful as a magnet had drawn him to return to Philadelphia on his own, to visit the sailmaker and the Ellis family, asking and receiving their forgiveness, and to visit Independence Hall, because of what he had learned in the college library. And he told about the first time he had gone alone to an anti-slavery rally, and of subsequent rallies he had attended in the intervening time.

Finally Fletcher conveyed to them how he had tried to bear the ambivalence he felt, until his realization of the ultimate significance of the Frederick Douglass letter had become a catalyst.

"Now I feel an aversion to slaveholding which has left me with no alternative to coming here to see you today." Hesitating, Fletcher clearly was emotionally drained. "I come to volunteer, sirs, to help in any way I can. So permit me to ask, what can I do to earn your trust?"

McDonald pressed a button. The black clerk appeared in the doorway. "Bring our North Carolina book."

"Yassuh, right quick."

The two older men did not look at each other; each remained deep within his own thoughts. The clerk returned and set the book on the director's desk.

Thumbing through the book, McDonald found a page, read for a moment, then glanced up at Fletcher.

"Your father's surname also is Randall, and your mother's first name is Ethel, is that correct?"

Fletcher's face was a study is astonished disbelief.

The director began calling names: "Ham, Lem, Caesar, Pompey, Rastus, Chloe, Liza, Luther—do you recognize any of those?"

"No, sir." Fletcher was puzzled.

"So you wish us to believe you're willing to risk your life to help black slaves, when you don't even recognize the names of your own slaves on the plantation you will inherit?"

Fletcher flushed at the barb, but he recovered. "You can't know the names of most of those you help either, can you?"

McDonald said, "Whom could we query about you—confidentially, of course? Your Quaker friends, for instance?"

"I would beg that they know nothing of this, sir, especially as one is my classmate." Fletcher hesitated. "But, sir, if you must, then of course you must. But believe me, I have come here by myself."

The director looked at the UGRR chief conductor, nodding at the door, and they both rose as McDonald said to Fletcher, "Will you excuse us for a moment?"

"Of course, sir."

Outside in the hallway, McDonald spoke in a low voice. "What do you really think?"

"Honestly, I am impressed. He's telling the truth, I do believe.

It's my first experience with such a young volunteer, but he's smart. He sounds to me capable."

The director said, "In there I was thinking that this young Southerner's background gives him the perfect disguise to be one of your agents."

"We were thinking exactly alike. But I'd want some more time just to mull this over—perhaps to test him somehow."

"Of course. There's no need to rush anything." McDonald reflected. "He's come here to us because we're public, but you know he's got the two of us confused."

"Obviously," said the conductor.

When the two men reentered McDonald's office, Fletcher was on his feet, studying the several framed portraits evenly spaced on the wall.

"Would you tell me who these are, sir? I need to know, if they're important enough to be hanging here."

The director said, "Yes, but my colleague is really the person to tell you about them."

The UGRR conductor walked over and pointed to the nearest portrait, a white man. "Seth Conklin volunteered and went South and rescued an escaped slave's wife and children. He was bringing them North but they were captured and Seth Conklin was found dead with his ankles and wrists chained and his skull fractured."

The UGRR conductor spoke as unemotionally as if he were giving a roll call. He indicated another white man's portrait. "Captain Lee was caught rowing four slaves hidden in the bottom of a skiff. He was tried, convicted, and sentenced to five lashes daily for ten days before he was taken to the Richmond Penitentiary to serve twenty-five years. That's where he died."

At the next portrait, a black man: "This free Negro, Robert Purvis, and other abolitionists organized the Vigilance Committee in 1838."

The next face, a white: "We call the Quaker named Levi Coffin the President of the Underground Railroad," said the UGRR conductor. "He was born in 1789 in your State of North Carolina, where he saw and hated cruelty to slaves, and in 1826 he moved to Indiana, then in 1847 to Cincinnati, where in his home he assisted over one hundred slaves to escape each year."

Then came a black woman's face. "She's Harriet Tubman, who escaped, and she has devoted her whole life to returning South, time and again, and bringing out others who by now have amounted to more than one hundred. She is known as the Moses of her people."

The director of the Vigilance Committee tapped his fingers against the other framed portraits, only calling their names. "Thomas Garrett, Henry Bibb, William Still—" He looked at Fletcher. "You told us you knew this one, Frederick Douglass."

McDonald paused. He said to Fletcher, "Before you leave, we think you have our agencies confused."

Fletcher was puzzled. "How, sir?"

"Our work in the Vigilance Committee is principally providing food, clothing, legal help, and survival money for those slaves who have already made it North." He indicated the UGRR conductor. "You should know my colleague here."

"I am Clay Marlon, the Underground Railroad chief conductor, and Mr. McDonald and I work together closely."

Fletcher's eyes met the UGRR chief conductor's. "I am honored, sir."

"My pleasure," said the chief conductor. They shook hands firmly.

The chief conductor studied Fletcher carefully. "Let me stress the message of those portraits, young man. Our work does not involve any schoolboy escapades. Also, being one of our white agents does not offer protection against being dealt with as brutally as the blackest of escaping slaves. We have had agents beaten, tortured, and murdered, believe me."

"Yessir."

McDonald glanced again at his clock. "Young man, you do impress us more than we would have thought. And you will be contacted if and when we feel we need you."

It was during their mid-October meeting when the chief conductor of the Underground Railroad next spoke of Fletcher to the director of the Philadelphia Vigilance Committee.

"We naturally had to find out more about the young man, which has come now from a friend of ours in administration at the college. Although his response isn't conclusive, young Fletcher Randall's story does seem to check out."

He handed over a folded notepaper, which McDonald read quickly.

"Sounds convincing to me," said the director.

"I believe him. I like him, too."

"I just hate to think of him so young out on a mission, if he'd get caught, you know?"

The UGRR chief conductor looked solemn. "I do have a mission for him. Very special."

Quickly he described it. McDonald puffed his cheeks and exhaled.

"Well, what do you think?" Marlon asked.

McDonald paused a moment. "I think I'd send a message to your new agent to report here next Saturday morning."

As expected, Fletcher reported, filled with tension. He had not entirely recovered from the shock he'd experienced the previous Wednesday when, walking along a campus sidewalk, he'd become aware of the man close beside him, matching his steps. Then he'd heard the words, spoken softly yet distinctly, "Report Saturday morning to the Philadelphia office. Do you understand?"

Nearly stumbling from surprise, Fletcher had managed a muffled "Yes," whereupon the man turned and left in the opposite direction. Fletcher never had really seen his face.

But the incident had served to reaffirm what he had been told, that he had volunteered himself into some serious business.

As he had anticipated, Fletcher found both the UGRR's chief conductor and the Vigilance Committee director in the office. As soon as the self-important black clerk ushered him in, the director motioned him to a straight chair close by the desk, which held a lined white paper tablet, pen, and inkwell.

The UGRR's chief conductor said, "Now, Fletcher Randall, I will dictate slowly and clearly for you the Underground Railroad Membership pledge. You are to take your time, writing it legibly in your own hand."

"Yes, sir."

The pledge was just under a page in length. When Fletcher finished, Marlon said, "Beneath that, add your full signature if you will."

After Fletcher signed, Marlon produced a saucer holding a

small folded cloth that was dampened with black ink. "Please, your right thumb?"

Taking Fletcher's thumb, the chief conductor pressed it down hard against the inked cloth, then immediately against the tablet paper half an inch to the left of Fletcher's signature. Fletcher raised his hand. The black thumbprint was graphic.

McDonald handed him a kerosene-soaked cloth, and the two men watched him clean his thumb as if they were uncertain which of them would talk first. And both men were wondering how Fletcher was going to react when he realized that his impending assignment was to be vastly more personal than he ever could have imagined.

His thumb mostly clean, Fletcher looked at them both.

Conductor Marlon spoke first.

"Normally, after signing our pledge, recruits are given at least a week to reconsider—"

"I won't need that," Fletcher interrupted sharply.

"Then I won't mince words." The UGRR chief conductor looked intently at Fletcher. "Do you feel prepared to take on a mission within your own home area? A mission that involves rescuing slaves from planters you personally know?"

Fletcher swallowed hard. "Yes, sir."

"Then, all right; we have decided to gamble on you. This is a mass escape mission, long in the planning, but only last week our key agent fell sick and can't continue, so you'll be his substitute. You've already arranged for your Christmas student vacation, have you not?"

"Yes, sir. I have three weeks, from the first December weekend through the Monday after New Year's."

"Good!"

Chief conductor Marlon stood as if to leave. "I regret I must hurry off. We're expecting a party of escapees to arrive by noon." He shook hands with Fletcher. "Be here this same time next week. By then I'll be able to give you full details of your mission."

"Yes, sir."

The Vigilance Committee director spoke quickly. "It goes without saying that you will have all our prayers and blessings, and as much support as we can humanly give."

"I thank you, sir." Fletcher hesitated. He looked at the UGRR chief conductor. "One more question, sir?"

"Yes, of course—"

"You said I'm to replace a key agent. Does that mean I function on my own, alone?"

Chief conductor Marlon looked at Fletcher. "Am I your brother?"

"Pardon me, sir?"

Director McDonald echoed, "Am I your brother?"

Fletcher stared at them both, confused.

"Whoever next asks you that question, in *exactly* those words, you will know is our trusted conductor permanently on duty in your assignment area," the chief conductor said. "You will work with him hand in hand, combining your special abilities with his to the fullest. Obviously we trust you, but you must appreciate that in the interest of complete security, we must keep his identity protected until you actually meet physically. At that time, take my word for it, you'll understand better."

The director of the Vigilance Committee and the chief conductor of the Underground Railroad exchanged strong handshakes with Fletcher Randall, who had seen no need to mention that it was his twentieth birthday.

V

*P*ARTLY BECAUSE the stocky, sooty-black Old Moses had variously assisted his massa and missis's extra-special preparations for their beloved Fletcher's Christmas 1855 homecoming, and partly because Old Moses had been so proud to be entrusted with actually picking up the young Massa, as he turned the two pedigreed mares drawing the buggy into the long maple-lined lane toward the magnificent white-columned mansion, he jubilantly spanked the reins against the mares' chestnut rumps, and they quickly advanced to a gallop, abruptly causing Fletcher and his two pieces of luggage to jounce around in the rear seat.

The speeding buggy was still some distance away, just entering the gentle bend of the lane, when it was seen by Mandy, the missis's faithful upstairs maid. *"Massa! Massa! Missis! Missis!"* For the past two hours, bundled up against the cold, she had hung about the front veranda for the excitement of shouting out that first sighting. And now she'd been rewarded.

Old Moses' strident *"whoas!"* slowed the spirited mares, and the buggy came coasting onto the curving driveway amidst the mansion's expansive flowered and hedged front lawn. But before the buggy stopped, Fletcher leaped out and into the arms of his parents, who embraced him wildly. They were so filled with love and pride of him, they had for so long hungered for their next sight of him, that it was several minutes before they finally released him to the frantic huggings and cheek-kissings and pummelings from the trusted Big House slaves—Mandy, his mother's personal "jewel"; Liza Mae, the downstairs maid who also served the dining table; Maella, the mulatto weaver and seamstress who made his and his father's shirts; Peter, the gardener; Cairo, the stablekeeper; and of course Old Moses—who had anxiously bunched behind their senior, the ageless cook Hattie, to await their turns at greeting Fletcher.

All during the fervor of the greetings, no one would have noticed if Fletcher had shouted out his suddenly overwhelming feelings of ambivalence. "Oh, my Lawd, you's jes' growed on up so pretty!" crowed Hattie, who had tended him as a little boy. "An' Lawd done heared my prayers git you home je's right on time for dinner!" Hattie laughed triumphantly, and then Mandy screeched, "Hattie been three days fixin' you dinner, Massa Fletcher!" Fletcher had made a critical pledge to help slaves find freedom—but he thought it could not include these who so obviously would shun it, who so clearly saw themselves as faithful members of the Big House family. Fletcher realized with dismay that if they knew about his mission, they would consider him a traitor.

Traditionally, preceding dinner the senator solemnly said grace, upon this occasion thanking a bountiful God for bringing the family together again after so long a time. Then Liza Mae passed to Fletcher a covered shiny container whose top he lifted—and he whooped with laughter, remembering how many countless boyhood autumn and winter mornings he had been awakened by that same heavenly aroma, and snatching on his clothes had gone flying downstairs nonstop into Old Black Hattie's cookhouse out back where she would quickly butter for him some of the hot yeast rolls barely out of her old hickory-fire oven.

And what followed was a triumph of Hattie's memory of the dishes that Fletcher had always especially loved. Her onion-gravied fried chicken vied with the smothered rabbit, and her sausage dumplings competed with the baked corn custard and the sweet-potato puffs, even as her winter-canned mixed mustard and turnip greens rivaled the whippoorwill peas with fatback. Finally Liza Mae, who couldn't hold back her grinning with the meal's success, brought in the dessert—Hattie's indescribable papershell pecan pie, hidden totally from sight under her mounded slightly sweetened whipped cream.

When his father had smiled over a forkful of the whippoorwill peas and asked, "Well, tell us, Mr. Junior, how goes life at college?", with relief Fletcher had answered, "Well, about the college itself, Dad, I can't praise it enough. Yale and Harvard both have outstanding special departments. But so have we in Princeton. And in general, none can be called better."

Fletcher buttered his fifth light yeast roll and continued, "My biggest problem, same as I told you when I was home last Christmas, is some of the damned Yankees—"

He watched his father quit chewing at mere mention of the word. Knowing what reassurance and gratification he could give, Fletcher verbally flayed most Yankees he had encountered directly, especially Tom Barrett, Peter Estabrook, Edgar Ascot, and Williams Gaines.

Senator Randall smiled, nodding at his wife. "Well, hon, we can be mighty proud and glad; we seem to have won the gamble. The South has got to gamble and enroll a whole lot more of our young coming leaders in those Northern colleges to study and learn the Yankee's ways and bags of tricks."

Mrs. Randall leaned over to touch Fletcher's hand. "What I'm glad about is, our son's home," she said. "My baby, what courses are you taking that you maybe haven't mentioned in your letters?"

"Well," Fletcher said, "one course I especially liked is called moral philosophy—"

He saw his mother's eyebrows rising. "Well, I guess it could be described as studying what seemed to be the essentials of Christian living."

"Oh yes, I see," said Mrs. Randall, patently impressed.

Fletcher said, "One thing for certain, the professor who teaches it is the one I like the most among all my others at Princeton— Dr. C. Erick Lincoln, a Southerner, too, from Memphis. I checked his biography in the library, and he studied under England's famous Dr. Hampden, at Oxford."

Mrs. Randall smiled. "Darling, it pleases me *so* much that you're continuing to make good use of a library."

Fletcher gestured a salute. "One guess—my lifetime influence?"

They all three laughed, and the temporarily overlooked Senator Randall sought a topic more to his interest. "Fletcher, would you care to describe, well, the political climate at the college?"

Fletcher laughed. He would divert that one. "My politickings mostly are at the female academy up the road."

"Just don't do anything I wouldn't," the senator chuckled.

Mrs. Randall groaned, "I'd say that gives him far too much leeway."

She touched the mother-of-pearl button atop her small silver table bell, and its clear tinkling brought Liza Mae practically on the run.

Mrs. Randall told her, "Come with me into the living room to open the wines and arrange things so our talking can continue in there."

Randall had sprung up to pull back his mother's chair. After she went out, the senator bent near. "My boy, you're grown, I know, but I offer some good advice anyhow. Whenever you feel like tomcatting, find you fifty or seventy-five cents' worth of real nice mulattoes or high-yellows. I'm told they can be hot as firecrackers, and I'm sure they're running around loose up there among the Yankees just like they are around here." He winked at Fletcher. "What I mean is, save the seriousness for marrying."

Fletcher's mind flashed to the sundry mulattoes, octoroons, quadroons, and high-yellows he had seen paraded onstage in Philadelphia as recently escaped fugitive slaves, often testifying that their masters were their fathers, if indeed their complexions had required that testimony. In his dormitory room he had thought a great deal about how the so-called "patriarchal institution" annually cursed new thousands, both male and female, with those near-white complexions and a slave's status.

As Fletcher's mother reappeared in the doorway, smiling at them, beckoning them to join her in the living room, he thought that his ordeal of having rejected the kind and gracious Quakers was as nothing compared to coming home to betray his parents, who had given him life.

He vividly recalled the grave expression of chief conductor

Marlon in Philadelphia when he gave Fletcher the final orders to share with his as yet unknown fellow agent.

"We don't put our orders in writing, so listen carefully. Memorize what I say and repeat it back to me when I finish. In Ashe County you and your contact will combine your ingenuity and your knowledge of the locality to initiate the escape of twelve fugitives—at least six from your area's largest slaveholder, Senator Randall." The conductor said the name matter-of-factly, and Fletcher had managed to accept it without flinching. "You'll see to it that this party is given safe passage through the thick forest route in time to arrive before daybreak at the home depot of UGRR stationmaster Quaker Evans. You'll advise your party in advance that Quaker Evans will hand them over to the next agent, who'll lead them to Appalachian limestone caves in the area, where they'll hide during the day and travel at night, following the North Star to Philadelphia."

Fletcher repeated these instructions several times, until Marlon was satisfied that they were indelibly etched in his mind.

Conductor Marlon had looked into Fletcher's eyes. "This order specifies your father, so I must know—have you any reservations?"

Fletcher had heard his voice say, "I am pledged to follow orders, sir."

"I realize this is a terrible challenge for a recruit," Marlon said. "A huge responsibility. But I think I can read people. And I read you as being up to this. I read you as being not a boy but a man. That's what I'm counting on."

The orders had been much less specific than Fletcher had anticipated, leaving him and his companion agent largely to their own devices, but when Fletcher considered how many variables such a mission could involve, he understood why. And he was emboldened by conductor Marlon's faith in him.

And then, traveling homeward for Christmas, Fletcher had realized that he was a criminal: in having expressed his intent to break the law of the land, he was subject to arrest, prosecution, conviction, imprisonment—and if he got caught by some of the vicious slavecatchers hired by slaveholders like his father, he could lose his life.

As he entered the well-appointed family living room he noticed a leatherbound copy of Sir Walter Scott's *The Heart of Midlothian* on a table. Fletcher's mother loved Scott passionately, indiscriminately, as did many in the South. He remembered her reading Scott to him when he was a child. And *The Heart of Midlothian* was her favorite of all Scott's novels, because it featured a character she adored—Jeanie Deans, a humble lass whose courage and unassuming faith she found inspirational.

Fletcher felt his mother gently take his arm, and her voice was soft and caring. "Darling, your mind sometimes seems to be elsewhere. We know you're exhausted from traveling, and you need to rest. Just try to bear with us a little while, darling. Understand that we're rooted here on this big ol' plantation, where nothing much ever seems to happen, and your father's gone half the time attending the legislature. That's why we're both so hungry to share some of your experiences away from us at your college."

He was jolted. He hadn't dreamed that his distractedness could be so apparent. Bracing his mind to concentrate more intensely, he hugged his mother, managing a laugh. "Yes, ma'am, all that traveling sure has worn me down—" He patted his stomach. "Plus I just ate at least twice too much."

His mother accepted it, and as soon as they were seated with their wines served by Liza Mae, Mrs. Randall renewed the conversation. "Darling, tell us how you spend your weekends."

Fletcher said that he usually did lone field trips designed to broaden and enrich his personal experience. He did not tell a lie in never mentioning the Quakers, or uttering so much as one syllable about the city of Philadelphia.

After his mother had plied him with her saved-up questions, Fletcher saw her stifle a yawn. He bent forward, tension and excitement gathering in his manner and voice. "Back in Princeton, I've been thinking—you all want to hear a fantastic idea? Why don't we throw a truly different Christmas Eve celebration, to knock everybody on their heels! Let's give a big barbecue party. And combine it with a homecoming festivity!"

He could see they didn't understand. He knew that a state senatorial election was coming up soon, and although his father was not worried about losing, he would dearly love to win once again in a very big way.

So Fletcher bore down with details of how an apparent Christmas Eve homecoming for himself could also serve as a highly dramatic and effective political stratagem. "I mean, having Old Mose, Peter, and Cairo, all three, riding out on horseback to deliver our invitation will give us not only the season's major social event, but also a senatorial reelection campaigning coup."

The senator sprang up from his chair. He had taken to the idea like a hungry catfish. "Marvelous, *magnificent!*" He went over and slapped Fletcher on the back.

But Mrs. Randall sounded appreciably less sure. "But it's only two weeks to Christmas! Isn't there too little time left to arrange all this?"

"We'll handle it, just don't you worry!" Senator Randall exclaimed. "At the cotton gin, we'll get enough canvas to tack onto a two-by-four foundation all around our veranda like a big tent! And we'll heat it with as many small stoves as we need. Why, it'll be no problem at all! And I guarantee you that nobody in the world can do more with the barbecuing end of things than Harpin' John. He's just the best there is, that's all, you know that!"

"Well, all right, if you're so sure—"

"Of course, I'm sure, my dear! Now, your job is to make up an exclusive invitation list, everybody who's important!"

Mrs. Randall said, "Well, you both know I'll do all I can. But just remember, it's you two big headstrong grown-up boys' barbecue party."

The more Senator Randall visualized it, the more excited he got.

He jabbed his finger at Fletcher. "No time to waste, son. First thing tomorrow, you ride over to Tom Graves's place—you need to hire the whole Christmas-season time of his slave barbecue man, Harpin' John. You know, the one who goes around playing his darky music on a harmonica all the time."

The serving maid, Liza Mae, entered the living room with coffee cups, sugar, and cream weighing down her tray.

"I don't think I remember having heard of him," Fletcher said.

"Between the academy and now college, son, you've been away for most of the time since you were fourteen," Mrs. Randall said. She yawned again, seriously this time. She pushed herself upright. "I'm just too drowsy from the sherry to enjoy any coffee, Liza Mae," she said, and then, turning, "if you all will excuse me, please, my big strong men, I'm going upstairs and get some rest."

She made a mock curtsy to them both. "It sure sounds as if, starting tomorrow, we're all about to have some mighty busy days."

Her husband and son responded with gallantly formal bows from their waists. Smiling back at them, Mrs. Randall disappeared toward the upstairs.

The senator went and stood over the oblong polished oak wine table. He poured them both another port and waved the back of his hand toward Liza Mae, who fled.

Fletcher took his glass of port. "Thanks, Dad," and then, "we've talked enough about me. So why don't I hear how everything's going for you all down here at home?"

Senator Randall sipped his port before he sat back down. Then he sipped again. "Well, considering all, things are going quite well, I'd say. We've harvested a pretty good crop, both the cotton and tobacco."

The senator sipped again. "Purchasing prices for slaves are getting better—the supply is exceeding the demand. Around here nowadays you can pay under a thousand for a pretty useful male, and only last week I bought a woman with child able to work for even less."

"I see," Fletcher said. His flinching went unnoticed.

"The same damned Yankees are our South's major problem." Senator Randall warmed to his topic. "It's not enough that they pay too little for the sweat and labor of our agricultural products. Now these despicable creatures are circulating all over around here, using all sorts of occupational disguises to work for an anti-slavery organization, and also this Underground Railroad as they call it. Son, I mean even some well-raised native Southern whites have been corrupted by the Yankees."

Both Fletcher and his father bottoms-upped their port glasses, then each poured himself another. The senator was truly fired up. "Yankees have got to get it into their heads that the South's real sick of having hundreds of thousands of dollars' worth of slave properties kidnapped and led off to some 'freedom' that blacks by their very nature have not the faintest idea what to do with!"

Senator Randall quaffed.

"I tell you, my boy, sitting and listening as I do in our state's legislature, I know what I'm talking about. Let the Yankees keep up their damn dirty tricks and you watch: four, five years from now, we'll see a war of secession! I mean the Southern states will leave the Union before we'll give up our slaves!"

To stifle his father, Fletcher abruptly asked him a question. "Can you fill me in a bit more, Dad, about this barbecue man's master I'm to go see first thing tomorrow?"

"You're right," Senator Randall said, "you do need to know more than I've told you. Again, Tom Graves is his name. He's not a real planter, nowhere compared to our class. He's a lucky redneck, but give him credit, he worked his tail off to finally buy a small farm. Then his real luck came when he bought cheap this black slave family whose oldest child grew up into Harpin' John, and he's just absolutely the greatest barbecue man in these parts—anybody you ask will tell you that—not to mention the almighty best harmonica player anybody ever heard of! So you see, the situation in a nutshell is you're going to meet and make a deal with this redneck master, Tom Graves, to let you hire out his gifted black slave—"

"Fine and dandy!" Rising, stretching, Fletcher said, "But I'm going to need a good night's sleep. And you look like you could use some rest, too, Dad."

Senator Randall swirled his glass. "You go on ahead, son. I'll just sit here for a while and savor that plan of yours. By damn, you're going to make a hell of a politician yourself one of these days!"

Alone in his room, Fletcher was assaulted with nostalgia. Hanging on a wooden peg was the worn, faded, and frayed little rectangular blanket that as a toddler he'd dragged about behind him everywhere, hollering and yelling in outrage when Black Hattie, then younger, would take it away to be washed. His old torn, discolored, and unraveling toy bear sat propped up forlornly in a corner with one of its brown glass eyes dangling by a string. His three baseball bats of varying girths and lengths were stacked neatly on the floor beside the chest of drawers on top of which was a green glass dish containing numerous smaller mementos.

Looking at these childhood relics reminded him of his favorite playmate, Hattie's black son, nicknamed "Rabbit" because he ran so fast. "Rabbit" was almost the same age as Fletcher. His special status as Fletcher's friend spared him from working as a field hand.

They were about ten or eleven when they had both caught a burning fever. Fletcher could only dimly remember Hattie's black face, so full of love and care, peering down at his fevered forehead by day and by candlelight as she placed cool damp rags on his forehead. And then, when he finally recovered, he'd been taken to see the flat round rock which marked Rabbit's place under the recently mounded earth in the plantation's slave graveyard.

Fletcher wondered why it had not occurred to him until now that Hattie might have saved her son by spending more time nursing *him*. And Rabbit would now be tending the yard, or the garden, or the barn, because Hattie as the cook would wield enough influence to keep her son from slaving under the hot sun in the tobacco and cotton fields.

Fletcher told himself that now his secret, dangerous objective was to try and help other Rabbits escape into freedom and a better life in the North.

After an hour in bed, Fletcher couldn't sleep, even exhausted as he was. The secret password felt branded into his brain. But when was the companion agent going to appear? And who was he? He could be any man among the hundreds his father said were moving about the South. Wealthy planter parents, for instance, hired their children's special tutors, and teachers of music and the dance, from the North, and from Europe. Clowns, jugglers, actors, for whom traveling was a way of life, might easily function as UGRR agents, entirely unsuspected.

And then Fletcher remembered things he had heard of agents who had been unlucky enough to get caught. Their deaths had been horrible. And he did not doubt what he had heard, for years before, one weekend when he had come home from the academy a small outbreak of slave escapes had occurred, and Fletcher remembered how he had been taken aback to hear the depth of bitterness, fear, and loathing expressed by his own father and other planters who met at their mansion and bluntly described what they wanted done to anyone, especially anyone white, caught assisting slaves to get away.

Fletcher was doing his utmost to force out of his mind that which he simply could not willingly bring himself to face—the agony of betraying the love and the trust of his mother and father.

And lying across his bed now, he knew that if this was the

emotional price for only a part of his first day at home, the truth was that he might not be able to go through with his assignment. Had he the right to act against the convictions of his mother and father because *he* had come to believe so passionately that freedom was the due of black slaves?

Fletcher's mind went back to the pledge he had signed and then sealed with his inked thumbprint. He wondered, wildly now, what would happen if he apprised chief conductor Marlon that upon returning home after a year away and reexperiencing the warmth of family life, being only human and possessed of unpredictable frailties, he had changed his mind.

Could he make the UGRR compromise instead? Could he offer to donate to their goals the trust fund from his mother's father which would be legally his at the age of twenty-one? His parents would not necessarily have to know what he had chosen to do with those funds. But how would Vigilance Committee director McDonald and chief conductor Marlon react? Would they find it within themselves to understand, and to forgive?

That would be the ultimate crucifixion.

No, he couldn't risk that.

Fletcher lay there across his bed, wallowing in an agony of indecision. It was nearly daybreak when he realized that his lips were moving, soundlessly shaping the words of Frederick Douglass, which he had indelibly memorized: "No rich, no poor, no high, no low . . . No black, no white . . . But one country, one citizenship, equal rights . . . And a common destiny for all . . ."

Fletcher got out of bed and knelt to pray. He prayed that his assignment be accomplished without the loss of a single life. He prayed that if he might be blessed to see this one mission accomplished, he would never again betray his parents.

VI

*A*WAKENED BY persistently chirruping birds, Fletcher washed and dressed and hurriedly made his way downstairs, through the mansion and out back into the cookhouse, where, as he anticipated, Old Black Hattie was already stirring and had the coffee ready. He insisted on pouring a cup for himself, then sat straddling a straight chair with its back facing Hattie's cooking table, and said, "Fix me some bacon and eggs fast as you can. I've got to ride over and see the master of somebody we need to hire called Harpin' John."

Old Hattie started thick slices of bacon frying in her heavy black cast-iron skillet. "Yassuh, Liza Mae what served y'all last night done already tol' me 'bout that big barbecue party, suh, an' b'lieve me, it gonna take every day of fixin' for jes' the barbecuin' for that big night."

Hattie paused. "Massa, sump'n I ought to tell you, since you be traveling places. You know Ol' Mose what brought you home in the buggy—well, last night he come down pretty bad off sick. Don't know what it is exactly, but he sho' be in dat bed for a while yet. We takin' care of him all right enough."

"Sorry to hear that," Fletcher said. "So, tell me, you know this Harpin' John?"

"Oh, my Lord, everybody do! Ain't much excitin' gits put on in this county, 'specially in the way of a big barbecue whoop-de-do, without Harpin' John. He jes' the best barbecuer they is, everybody know that. Or whatever big house give a big cotillion party, he be right there playin' the fool out'n his harmonica! He ain't never married nobody yet, an' ain't never no tellin' what pretty gal at whose planatation he runnin' after. But jes' 'bout everybody know Harpin' John like him, he jes' so full of fun an' carryin' on."

Cracking three eggs into a bowl, whipping them vigorously with a wooden fork for soft scrambling, as she remembered Fletcher liked them, she beamed at her private appreciation of Harpin' John.

"What about this Tom Graves, his master?"

Hattie hesitated. "Ain't gonna tell you nothin' but truth. Big massas like yo' daddy done spoilt that po' redneck, invitin' him and his po' l'il ol' scrawny-built wife to come where they hire Harpin' John to play. So Massa Tom Graves and his wife, they think they up in y'all's society where they ain't got no business nohow!" Hattie stirred the eggs being scrambled. "Now I ain't gonna say no more, 'cause I ain't s'posed to git into no white folks' business."

After breakfast, Fletcher mounted his horse which the sta-bleman, Cairo, had saddled and ready. He cantered down the long, maple-lined lane and shortly was on the dirt main road. His jaw was set. Hiring the black musician and barbecue man was secondary. His principal concern, which nagged at him considerably, was how soon his yet unknown UGRR partner would make contact. Fletcher was tensely half-expecting the sound of a horse approaching from behind, whose rider would nudge up closely and say the magic words. For time was critical to the organization of a hopefully unsuspected mass escape while the slaveowner planters were drinking and feasting on Harpin' John's legendary barbecue.

And, Fletcher thought, he had to find some way to circulate Christmas gift bottles of whiskey to overseers, who were bound to get drunk, knowing that their masters were at the party.

Every so often Fletcher was waved at by people also out early along the road, on horses or in their buggies, and he either slowed down or stopped, depending upon whether or not he recognized them.

He noticed that each time a vehicle either slowed down or stopped with its white passengers waving at him and calling greetings, the black driver always sat up on his high seat like a statue, looking straight ahead. Fletcher wondered if some of them had escaping on their minds.

The Tom Graves plantation was modest by average planter standards, and the house where Graves and his wife lived was quite small. Fletcher would have expected a lucky redneck to have risked bankruptcy to build at least a small mansion with which to show off. And Tom Graves, in the tradition of many poor whites, had ten or twelve hound dogs lying around in the front yard, three or four of which rose and barked. Fletcher dismounted, thinking that at least he liked the honesty and unpretentiousness of Tom Graves, who came outside and in a gangling way approached his visitor at the gate.

When Fletcher introduced himself as Senator Randall's son, Tom Graves all but prostrated himself. "Yes, I heard about you doing so fine at the big college up North." He swallowed, and his Adam's apple bobbed. "I believe your daddy's the finest man this county's got, no question about it!"

During the next few minutes of obligatory Southern chitchat before any business talk, Fletcher heard about the recent weather, the laziness of slaves, and so on. It was transparent, as Hattie had said, that Tom Graves lusted to appear important, and that he would stand on his head to do anything he could for one so powerful as Senator Randall.

Fletcher said that his father wished to hire the slave Harpin' John to stage a giant Christmas Eve barbecue on their mansion's veranda. Tom Graves was vigorously nodding his head as Fletcher went on that the unusual wintertime barbecue would be the centerpiece for a different kind of Christmas party.

But when Fletcher remembered to specify Christmas Eve *night*, Tom Graves's long face blanched.

"Oh, Lordy!" Tom Graves wailed. "Oh, my Lord, *any* other night!" His tone and manner appealed for understanding. "Since two months, Harpin' John's been hired to play his harp for Melissa Anne Aaron's Christmas Eve church pageant they give every year!"

Fletcher vaguely remembered Melissa Anne Aaron, a class or so below him in the dame school he'd attended briefly before he went away to the academy—chubby, as he recalled, nothing special. He spoke as if he hadn't heard Tom Graves. "Well, my father says we've got to have your man—nobody else can stage what we want."

"Oh, Lordy!" Tom Graves looked stricken. "Nobody in this world I'd rather please than your daddy, the senator!" He clutched at his chin. "Maybe we can work something out, I just don't know."

Fletcher said, "We can't waste time. If it's all right with you, I'll ride on over right now and see Mr. Aaron."

"He's the one did the hiring," Tom Graves said hopefully.

"You sure do go with my hopes and prayers," he continued. They shook hands. Then, as Fletcher swung up onto his horse, Tom Graves called, "Now, please don't forget to give your daddy my hello!"

Merry harmonica music caught the ears of the old cook Hattie, who was seated on a low stool peeling white potatoes which she would boil and mash with butter and cream as a part of her menu for the Randalls' dinner. She got up from the stool smiling and went to the door, where she saw the high-stepping horse entering the Big House rear yard, its rider the characteristically irrepressible and resplendent Harpin' John; with one hand he held his harmonica cupped up against his mouth, and he was playing it hard. He wore his trademark broad-brimmed brown hat, his orange neck scarf, his tan suit, and his matching high-topped shoes.

When Hattie got into the cookhouse doorway, Harpin' John dismounted and he stuck the harmonica back into his pocket. "Hey, big pretty mama!" he called across to Hattie. "My massa found me and say your massa want me two places at once, playin' my harp and cookin' barbecue. Massa say for me to git over here real quick and see what they got worked out. What kind of foolishness they talkin' 'bout, anyhow? Barbecuin' for Christmas!"

Hattie said, "Chile, don't need but two words to 'splain the whole thing. White folks. Ain't never no telling what they try next—an' you knows that jes' good as I do."

Hattie looked at him as if in disbelief of his outfit. "Harpin' John Graves, the way you show off, if I was whichever gal you courtin' the most now, I'd jes' fairly knock your block off, you hear me!"

Harpin' John grinned. Hattie said, "Well, if my massa seen your'n, far as I know he was comin' right back home. I don't know how you missed him."

"Well, I know. He went from there to see Melissa Anne Aaron, 'cause her Daddy got me hired for the same Christmas Eve, to play for they pageant at they church. So I figgered best for me to come on here and wait until your massa get back. See what they git worked out."

Hattie said, "Well, something gonna work, 'cause my massa want it worked out. Melissa Anne gonna git mad, I know that, but her daddy ain't gonna mess with no senator, I bet you that."

Harpin' John looked about. "I hears that Melissa Anne got herself pretty good hooked on that new young preacher at they church."

"Yeah, and her daddy worried to death she might get crazy enough to marry, 'cause he know that preacher sho' could use some they money."

As longtime good friends, Harpin' John and Hattie, there in her familiar and comfortable cookhouse, gossiped thoroughly about the community's social and political topics of interest. After a while, Hattie looked through her window and said, "Hey, yonder come young massa!"

Harpin' John was standing out near the barnyard stump where

Fletcher dismounted, smiling at the black master cook and musician's rainbow attire. "Your master tells me he's agreeable to our sharing you with the Aarons and their church on Christmas Eve night. I've asked Miss Aaron to start right on time and then when you play your last harmonica note you can grab your horse and ride fast to our place here to start serving up your barbecue."

Harpin' John grinned. "Suh, sho' sound like I gonna have a mighty busy night."

Fletcher said, "Oh, yes, one more thing for you. Maybe Hattie told you our driver Mose is down sick. Your master said it would be fine for you to drive me to take Miss Aaron to the cotillion at John Rice's plantation tonight. I hope maybe sometime during the drive we can get a chance to talk some more about the barbecue."

Harpin' John's heart sank. His master, Tom Graves, obviously had either forgotten or, in deference to the senator, had reneged on his promise that Harpin' John would have a free weekend, which he had earmarked for some important private visits.

Randall had considered that perhaps a romantic public image with the well-known young and pretty Melissa Anne could be most useful to allow him freer range of movement during the holidays. People would assume that he was busy courting.

Harpin' John thought to himself, Well, leave it up to her daddy, y'all jes' well make up a bed in the back of the carriage, much as her daddy love to add you to they family. But what he said aloud was, "Yassuh, and I 'gree we find any chance, you sho' could tell me some more details about this great big barbecuin' y'all wants."

When Harpin' John went back into the cookhouse and Hattie

caught a glimpse of his face at a certain angle, she stopped, puzzled. "Harpin' John, something ailin' you? Is anything wrong?"

"Naw, nothing!" He turned around and went back outside, with Old Black Hattie staring after him.

Dusk was approaching when Fletcher arrived at the Aarons' mansion, driven by Harpin' John in the senator's fine four-seater landau. He was greeted warmly and graciously by the master and mistress, who hastened him inside into their drawing room.

Mr. Aaron assured Randall of his pleasure with the compromise, for he personally loved the idea of a Christmas barbecue! "My boy, you and your daddy will be bringing off the biggest *do* of its sort within the history of this Ashe County!"

When Melissa Anne made her deliberately delayed and carefully practiced descent of the Aaron mansion's spiral staircase and then entered the drawing room, she extended her hand to Fletcher, whose expression told both her and her parents that she had achieved her loveliest. Her father already had dispatched their downstairs maid to tell Harpin' John to report to the front of the mansion with the landau.

The Aarons followed Melissa Anne and Fletcher outside and toward the carriage, whose door was held wide open for them by a Harpin' John standing ramrod-straight.

For just a fraction of a second, Mr. Aaron thought that the usually grinning and harmonica-playing Harpin' John seemed to be acting with an unusual solemnity instead of his special flair. Then, with the handsome young pair seated inside and Mr. and Mrs. Aaron waving and smiling, the landau began to move along its way to the main road, with some of the Big House window curtains pulled aside just enough to reveal the discreetly peeping approving black faces of Sukey and the other Aaron housemaids. As Fletcher and Melissa Anne engaged in an intermittent and rather awkward dialogue, Harpin' John, stiffly erect on the high driver's seat, gave no hint that his practiced ears were picking up every word they said.

They had rolled along for about a mile when Melissa Anne said, "If you're thinking about talking to the driver about your barbecue party, go ahead, I really won't mind."

"That's not proper!" Fletcher exclaimed so curtly that Melissa Anne was taken aback. She sat awhile studying her hands, not certain that she should have agreed to this night's date. And up on the front seat, Harpin' John's face seemed as if it were congealed.

When they arrived at John Rice's mansion, the footmen helped them from the landau, and Fletcher held Melissa Anne by her arm as they entered the jostling and excited crowd of revelers. The dancing was already well under way within the Great Hall, where two black fiddlers were performing atop a small square raised platform, their bodies bobbing, weaving, bowing, as they paraded their joint skill at fiddling, along with "cuttin' de fool for de white folks."

Fletcher and Melissa Anne made a handsome couple as they were happily and profusely greeted among the mostly blueblood family guests, some their parents' age, others former schoolmates, most of whom they had known all of their lives. Everyone shared the community's pride that Fletcher was an outstanding student at the Northern college at Princeton.

Between all of the greetings, Fletcher kept his eyes glancing, scanning the Great Room male faces, particularly alert should anyone initiate direct eye contact. He thought there could hardly be a better concealment for some UGRR assignment partner than within this gathering of mainly slaveholder families and their young ones.

As Fletcher swept Melissa Anne into the dancing, she really did reflect a radiance. The pair seemed clearly to be friends who had grown up together and were just discovering each other as romantic young adults, loving their dancing, halting only as one tune ended, then awaiting the cavorting fiddlers' next tune.

Finally Fletcher permitted another young gallant to cut in and give a spin to Melissa Anne. He began moving about within the Great Room, enjoying backslapping reunions with some old school friends from the academy. And then the host's elegant-acting black butler appeared in his velvet coat. He gestured his wish to say something to Fletcher, who nodded, curious. The butler came closer and whispered in Fletcher's ear, "Master Randall, sir, I've been told that your driver tonight is Harpin' John, who's now out among the other drivers waiting in the backyard. We want to ask you, sir, would you have any objection to his playing his harmonica for our guests, just once?"

Fletcher was at first startled to be asked, but he had heard so much about Harpin' John's harmonica playing that he laughed. "Of course not!" He watched the butler hasten away through a rear doorway that led out to the backyard where all of the drivers for the party's guests would be gathered and waiting.

Then soon Fletcher was astonished at the ripple of applause that steadily grew among the guests in the Great Room. He'd had no idea that the black slave was so well known as a musician even at the Big House level. He stared, seeing entirely another Harpin' John, this one coming cockily striding through the guests with his harmonica cupped up against his face and playing short, explosive little warm-up riffs on his harmonica, which he apparently always kept in his pocket wherever he went.

As Harpin' John hopped up onto the small raised stage, the two fiddlers stepped down onto the floor to flank him, one fiddler on either side. And Harpin' John's harmonica music fairly erupted into a virtuosity that had Fletcher's mouth hanging open. Harpin' John's clenched fists cupped the small instrument tightly against his mouth; his eyes were squinched shut, and every one of his facial muscles was strained in the intensity of his playing, while his body jerked and twisted and writhed, accompanying the driving beat of his music. Fletcher had never seen anything even remotely like it, and then he was an instant part of the wave of applause, whistles, and cheers, and he rose with the others when Harpin' John stopped and bowed and then left the room as quickly as he had come.

It had been altogether a glorious evening for everyone present when Melissa Anne said to Fletcher that they should leave a little bit early, as they had quite a distance to go.

She did not want to give Fletcher the impression that she thought he might have some private courting talk on his mind. She had thought once, as they were dancing, what a coup her family would regard it if she and Fletcher should get together —which would mean that she would have to break the young parson's heart. But she thought that would just have to be dealt with if the situation presented itself. She knew she would thus certainly earn the undying approval of her father—and of her mother as well. And then Melissa Anne also thought that from her own point of view she probably would not be disappointed, either.

The velvet-coated butler stood with his vain elegance clearly showing behind his master and mistress, the night's hosts, as they bade good night to Fletcher and Melissa Anne. Then the butler walked them to the landau waiting in the front entrance where Harpin' John stood holding the door open.

"You were absolutely wonderful!" Fletcher exclaimed.

Harpin' John bowed slightly, his hand still holding the carriage door's handle. "I thanks you, suh," he said.

Homebound in the landau, Fletcher sat a little closer to Melissa Anne than he had before, and she didn't object. He gestured at the dark silhouette ahead of them up on the driver's seat. "I had no idea—did you know he could play like that?"

"Why do you think I got him hired to play for our church program?" she said.

"Well, that church music will be of an entirely different sort."

"It doesn't seem to make any difference to him." Fletcher thought about a Northern free black young man who had once performed at Princeton. He was born blind, but somehow learned to play a piano, and he could hear any classical pianist play any score only once, and then the blind black pianist would play it back from memory, just exactly as he had heard it.

He said, "They're really remarkable people, some of them."

Melissa Anne said, "I guess so, if you think of darkies as people."

Most of the rest of the way they sat close with their hands

loosely clasped. They both seemed to be immersed in replaying the events of the evening, or perhaps in considering the potentials of the future. And ahead of them, seated up on his high, narrow driver's seat, gripping the horses' reins, with his posture stiffly upright, Harpin' John drove along in the clear December moonlight with his face shining as if it had been cast in wax.

An oil lamp's flickering glow lighted the second-floor main bedroom window of the Aaron mansion as the landau arrived and stopped on the drive. Melissa Anne's father came downstairs, wearing his bathrobe over his shirt and pants and holding another lamp in his hand, and Fletcher helped Melissa Anne step down onto the ground. He apologized to Mr. Aaron for the lateness of the hour and bade goodbye to Melissa Anne, saying he hoped they could get together again soon.

She nodded, and then she stood there bathed in the moonlight, smiling her prettiest, as her father thanked Fletcher, shook hands with him, and then turned to accompany his daughter inside.

During the goodbyes, Harpin' John had gone to the mansion's backyard well and drawn a wooden bucket of water which he had hurried back for the horses to have a needed drink. The horses finished the water and Harpin' John reached down and got the bucket as Fletcher walked back toward the landau.

Fletcher said, "Your master, Tom Graves, told me he's instructed you to meet me and my father at our home about twelve o'clock tomorrow, to talk about organizing the barbecue. That means noontime, and I want you to be sure and be there."

Harpin' John quickly glanced at the still Big House of the Aaron family. Then he turned back and looked piercingly into Fletcher Randall's eyes. "Am I your brother?" he asked.

Fletcher Randall was staggered. He had to steady himself by grasping the top of the tall rear wheel of the carriage. He responded weakly, "I—I am your brother."

Grasping Fletcher's arm, Harpin' John physically helped him on up into the carriage.

Dazed, Fletcher sat back on the carriage's rear double seat as Harpin' John slapped the reins against the horses' rumps and the canopied carriage jerked into motion.

The pair of them could hardly have seemed less conspiratorial, rolling along in the senator's elegant carriage with Harpin' John seated properly erect upon the raised driver's seat and the popular young collegian, the son of wealthy and powerful Senator Randall, lounging comfortably in the rear seat.

Fletcher repeated from memory their special orders from chief conductor Marlon.

Harpin' John felt as if the very pores of his skin had begun to close as he realized the unbelievable risk assigned to him and the young white man, the brand-new, untried, untested product of a Quaker family's influence. With less than two weeks remaining, how on earth were they supposed to organize and bring off a mass escape of "a maximum twelve" to follow the North Star to safety and freedom!

As if reading Harpin' John's mind, Fletcher continued, "I thought it might be best to split the escape into two separate parties, leaving at different times," he said tensely.

Harpin' John studied his hands holding the horse's reins. "Well, since it look like we good as axin' to die, you got to start somewhere some listenin' to me—" And Harpin' John explained that one en masse escape might be slightly less hazardous.

Fletcher agreed that a single group could take full advantage of the element of surprise. Harpin' John added that among the potential escapees he had in mind there was only one who had some leadership experience, "a man what know the country around in these parts real good. Like the trail we gonna put this group on, well, this here man been ten or more years working in the woods to pick the best trees to make shingles out of, until he know that trail right down to the last coon track. So we can pretty much count on it that he'll lead 'em straight to that Quaker depot where they supposed to go."

Fletcher said, "I must be honest—I'm still trying to adjust, because quite frankly I'd expected someone white."

"Well, I sho' ain't. An' speakin' truth, I wouldn't of never picked you, neither. But now we stuck with one 'nother, we worry 'bout colors later. But right now we got to trust one 'nother."

Then Harpin' John cupped his harmonica to his mouth, playing a rollicking tune.

"I never knew anyone could make that kind of music on a harmonica," Fletcher said, settling back.

"Me neither when I got hold of one when I was six, an' I been playin' ever since." He looked at the small instrument. "This one my best tools in what you and me doin'."

"How do you mean?"

Harpin' John put the harmonica to his mouth again, and brought forth a vivid sound unmistakably suggesting the chuffing of a railroad locomotive gaining speed. Fletcher leaned forward astonished.

" 'Git on board, li'l chilluns,' that what that mean—somebody waitin' to escape," said Harpin' John. Then he switched to the soft strains of a black spiritual. "You know that song's name?" asked Harpin' John.

"Seems I've heard it, but I can't name it."

Harpin' John sang, " 'Steal away . . . Steal away to Jesus—' See? It's a old black folks' church hymn, that's all white folks knows if they hear it. But for black folks ready to escape, it mean now it's time to go. See, one day if I go ridin' 'round cuttin' the fool for folks to see, but bein' at the right times and places, just playin' a little bit of 'Steal Away,' then nobody couldn't never say I'd spoke a word, 'cause I hadn't. But my message got said." He turned about, looked at Fletcher. "You see how I mean?"

Abruptly dropping the harmonica back into his pocket, Harpin' John next cupped both hands up over his mouth and as his cheeks puffed, Fletcher smiled, recognizing the mournful sound.

"Hoot owl," Harpin' John confirmed. "Now that's my signal if ever one of us gits lost." He thought a moment. "Got to teach you to do the hoot owl, too, first chance we git. An' show you some places if we ever need to hide—'cause that could happen!"

Just before they reached the Randall mansion Harpin' John said, "I be here at twelve o'clock tomorrow, to start 'ranging that barbecue. Quick as you can, you got to git you and me clear of your daddy. 'Cause you and me sho' got a whole lot more talkin' to do."

VII

*T*HREE DAYS LATER, Senator Randall was surprised and a bit annoyed when Liza Mae, the downstairs maid, came and said that the plantation overseer, John Hawkins, had just dismounted his horse in the mansion's side yard. "He axin' me if my massa at home, and I told him I don't know, but I go see what Massa say."

Walking outside, the senator coolly acknowledged his overseer, for they had no appointment and he felt strongly that overseers and other poor whites definitely should be kept at their distance, lest they start thinking themselves equals.

The overseer knew this. Standing with hat in hand, uncomfortably fingering the brim, he said he had felt the senator would be pleased to hear how much of a good impression his son was making on the local slave patrollers.

"What are you talking about?"

Hawkins put his hat behind his back. "Sir, somehow I felt like he'd decided to do this just on his own, but I knew that if you knew you'd be proud."

Hawkins volunteered that Fletcher had spent most of the past three days riding his horse between the area's slave patrol stations.

"You don't say!" the senator exclaimed.

"Oh, yes, sir!" The overseer was overjoyed that his effort to ingratiate himself had paid off. "The patrol boys tell me he's real interested in studying everything about the patrol work, to get a better idea about how to tighten things up. They say he's plumb full of questions."

Senator Randall remembered, "First night the boy got home we talked late, and I did mention some local cases of slave escapes—but I had no idea in the world he took it that serious."

"Well, he sure did, sir! The patrol boys say he's got a little tablet full of notes and even some sketches he's made of what they've told him about this part of the county's roads, and creeks, and where the bridges cross, and things like that."

"Well, I'll just be damned! Wait until I tell his mother this! She's been disappointed that he hasn't been spending more of his holiday around home."

"Well, sir, I'm sure Mrs. Randall will be pleased to know the way y'all's son is working on it, and with his kind of brains, we won't probably see any more slaves escaping out of this part of the country for a real long time."

"I want to thank you, Hawkins," the senator said. "By God, soon as Fletcher comes home, I'm going to apologize. Hell, I hadn't questioned him about where he's been gone so much because, tell you the truth, I'd figured he was off somewhere doing some serious tomcattin'."

The overseer, grinning, scratched at his right ear. "No, sir. What he's doing is making some real good friends among the patrollers. They can't believe that your son, rich and educated as he is, even would talk with them. He's even volunteered to stand a few shifts, to experience for himself how the patrolling works."

Harpin' John walked rapidly before a row of slave cabins, then halted and squatted down facing a middle-aged mulatto man who sat on a low stump wielding a short-handled wooden maul against an iron wedge froe, splitting a sawed oak tree section into shingles and arranging them into piles a foot tall.

"How you doin', you an' your good-cookin' wife, Uncle Ben?" Harpin' John asked lightly.

Without looking up from his task, Uncle Ben replied, "Fair, fair, I reckon. We's jes' settin' in the cabin nights, a-waiting to hear some ol' hoot owl."

"Spec' you might hear one some these nights 'fore too long," said Harpin' John. He had been closely eyeing the elder man's thin, worn coat. Impulsively, Harpin' John took his own coat off. "Uncle Ben, I want you to take this here coat an' put it on, 'cause you ain't warm enough in what you got on. I know you ain't, an' I got plenty more."

Uncle Ben stopped making shingles long enough to glance sideways at the proffered coat. "Naw, thank you, son. That there coat too pretty for somebody like me to have on. You go offer it to some these young'uns round here, I bet you they snatch it!"

Harpin' John said, "Peoples say the truth 'bout you, that you as hardheaded as you hardworkin'. But I tell you something, I'm just as hard-headed as you, an' I'm gonna give this here coat to your wife Miss Emma and tell her to keep after you until you wear it."

Uncle Ben gave a grunt of amusement. "She got 'bout much chance of that as gittin' me to ride a pig sidesaddle."

"Well, all right, Uncle Ben, I'm going to drop it by with her, anyhow, and then like I told you, you be hearin' the old owl one these nights, an' I know you good an' ready to lead the chilluns of Israel."

Harpin' John accomplished about dozen other similar brief visits, riding his horse hard between four plantations. Late that day, he headed the tired horse toward Senator Randall's mansion. Also, he was as tired as the horse from needing to be everywhere at once, which made him hard to find anywhere for as much as a half hour at once. He was, for one thing, bustling about, contacting people to help him put on the Christmas Eve barbecue at the Randall mansion. "We got to keep them white folks eatin' an' drinkin' they heads off, long enough for our folks to escape," he thought to himself. And he also allowed himself to envision and relish his legendary barbecuing process. Naturally it began with his knowing how to choose the best quality of meats, which would be no small matter in this instance, since the Randalls wanted not only barbecued pork but beef, veal, and chicken as well. And then he would marinate his meat, soaking it for at least thirty-six hours in his private mix that featured twelve spices pounded into a paste with blackstrap sorghum molasses. Next he would place his preseasoned meat over the best hickory embers covered with a layer of ashes to keep the heat so low that it would be twelve to fourteen hours before the barbecue would be ready to shimmy on the bones. Harpin' John smiled to himself. That was only half of his secret. The other half was his own special-ingredient sauce that he cooked, simmering, for as much as twenty-four hours. Harpin'

John couldn't help delighting at how many times he had served endless lines of white or black people, all of them singing their praises of his barbecue. Some had returned for helpings as many as five times!

Harpin' John knew that Mrs. Randall planned to have two hundred paper sacks half filled with sand into which a lighted candle could be stuck, so that on the night of the party a long line of those flickering beacons would mark the curving lane and the drive right on up to the front door of the Randall mansion.

The barbecue would be lighted by sixty kerosene lamps suspended from a thick wire strung tightly below the eaves of the Randall veranda. Right now, Harpin' John urgently needed to inspect the wooden platform structure of two-by-four beams which would support the wide unrolled sheets of canvas from the cotton gin to enclose the veranda like a tent. All of the construction work was being done by four slave carpenters owned by a small planter who usually hired them out, but let them work for the senator as a favor. Harpin' John had personally designed the row of wooden serving tables beneath which were the shelves on which his barbecue and other victuals would be kept in readiness when it came time for the serving of a planned two hundred hungry guests.

But as Harpin' John approached the Randall mansion, he began to hear black voices singing a Christmas carol.

So, first, Harpin' John went over to the cookhouse to learn what was happening from old Hattie.

Hattie didn't wait for him to ask. Tilting her head toward the singing voices she said, "Oh, Missus done borrowed two or three of the best singers from some of their good friends' plantations. She got 'em out there practicin' to sing as part of y'all's

Christman Eve big do." Hattie spoke while carefully watching Harpin' John. She was sure she glimpsed a quick frown.

She eyed him again. "I need you to do me a favor. You travel around so much, you try to find me somewhere a good handful of Saint-John's-wort. I knows some folks I needs to make a special blessin'."

He said, absently, "All right, I find you some, somewhere."

Hattie said, "And long as you at it, pick me up two, three real big nice nutmegs, too, for me to grate and sprinkle on the Big House eggnog."

Hattie wasn't surprised when Harpin' John didn't respond. She saw him physically standing there, but could tell that his mind was off somewhere else. Hattie's sudden tartness bespoke the sincerity of her concern. "Harpin' John Graves! Now you can't be too careful, you hear me!"

Melissa Anne Aaron was so angry that she acted fit to burst. At the age of eighteen, for the first time in the eighteen months her parents had permitted her some limited semblance of courtship, she had experienced a date being canceled! Her father was urging her to calm herself, and to accept young Fletcher Randall's explanation that he was extremely embarrassed, but that earlier he had committed himself to join two patrolmen in walking their route designed to prevent slave escapes.

"I don't care—what does he care about catching slaves!" exclaimed a furious Melissa Anne. "I just passed time with him, anyway! It's Parson Brown I intend to marry!"

"Consider what you're saying, my dear," Mr. Aaron said in his most soothing tone. "You truly need to consider the material aspect of what station in life you'll enjoy hopefully for the rest of your life. Bluntly, my dear, Parson Brown is a fine, good man, there's no doubt of that. But he's ten years older than you, for one thing, and, even more important, he has nothing to offer you beyond a parson's salary. And, again bluntly, my dear, whoever will be young Fletcher Randall's wife can plan to be rich for the rest of her life. I don't think your being a Christian follower of Parson Brown asks you to overlook that."

He halted—because Melissa Anne had fled in tears.

December 18, 1855, one week before Christmas, the teenaged son of a plantation overseer was out hunting with his father's best dog. At noontime the boy returned home for lunch. The boy was recounting to his father how he'd failed to find anything to shoot, and he laughingly mentioned that once when he thought the dog had actually treed something, upon investigation it turned out to be nothing but a pile of old quilts and blankets concealed under a heap of dry brush in the bend of a small ravine.

The overseer stopped eating as his son talked. He waited until the boy finished before saying, "All right, let's go, take me straight to that spot."

By sundown the news was all over Ashe County that a boy hunter with a dog had stumbled upon a fresh pile of quilts and blankets concealed near a trail head. Obviously they were meant for slaves ready to escape, who would need quilts and blankets as they made their way to the even colder North. So by the purest chance, a major escape had been foiled.

As the news spread during the next day, all hell broke loose on the plantations of Ashe and the adjoining counties. Obviously, the escape would not have been haphazard; it had been very carefully planned.

The next afternoon twenty-eight enraged planters, carrying rifles, rode in from both Ashe and the adjoining counties to gather on the veranda of Senator Randall's mansion.

The senator himself was livid. He had insisted that Fletcher be present to experience the problems of planters directly. In brief, angry session, the planters vowed death to anyone discovered to be involved.

Clustering about a veranda table, each of the twenty-eight planters wrote their checks or signed their pledges which totaled a sum sufficient to pay for a quadrupling and otherwise strengthening of the Ashe County slave-escape patrol. The meanest, toughest, most darky-hating local overseer would be hired to be in charge, with full clearance to choose his own squads of mean, tough darky haters, heavily armed and accompanied by dogs.

The weekly newspapers would each be given large advertisements offering rewards never before paid for the capture and return of any escaped slaves—who would be taught a lesson.

The two unlikely UGRR agents calculated that their best camouflage, the one least likely to arouse suspicions, continued to be traveling where they could talk safely in the carriage along the open main road, presenting to everyone who saw them the image of the powerful, rich state senator's college son lolling comfortably in the rear seat and being driven wherever he wished to go by the widely recognized happy-go-lucky black slave, Harpin' John.

But now, even they had to pass the scrutiny of hard-eyed patrollers carrying deer rifles who seemed everywhere, and were often as not augmented by volunteering angry small planters.

In the pervasively ominous atmosphere, instinctively the UGRR pair compressed their urgent exchanges into the briefest possible time.

"How are we going to get them away in this kind of atmosphere?" Fletcher asked. "It's absolutely deadly! We've got no choice I can see but to delay long enough to let things cool off a bit."

"That ain't likely to be for a good long while," said Harpin' John. "I think we might can do it this comin' Christmas Eve night, like we been plannin'." He looked back and forth in all directions. "I been talkin' to some friends."

"*Friends!* You mean Quakers?"

"Naw, Quakers some the best friends we got, all right enough. But I been talkin' to some the local Indians."

Indians! Good Lord, yes, why not? Fletcher thought. Nearly all Indians had been removed to Oklahoma in the 1830s, but small remnants of their tribes had remained and were living all over North Carolina—all over the whole South, for that matter. Indians were masters of nature craft. They could track any man or animal, following signs no white man could detect. They could even see in the dark!

Harpin' John said, "Right this minute, it's two of them Indian friends hacking through thicket down the back side of the plantation. They hack a covered sort of trail that lead to the New River." He looked at Fletcher. "You know how the New River runs?"

"Northeast, the best I remember."

"You 'members right. One our Indian friends has 'greed to lead our party, in some of their canoes, and he'll get 'em safe and sound to the Quaker depot. That sound all right to you?"

Fletcher grinned. "It sounds just like our orders!" He had to marvel at Harpin' John's ingenuity. And at the astuteness of chief conductor Marlon and the Vigilance Committee's director, McDonald, in having chosen him.

"Oh, yeah, one more thing," Harpin' John continued. "The Indians say they ruther leave early in the night. That'll mean our folks will get off during the church pageant instead of like we planned later, during the barbecue party."

Fletcher looked concerned.

"Don't worry, 'cause Indians know what they doin'."

VIII

*D*URING THE Christmas Eve lunchtime, Melissa Anne Aaron hotly challenged her father's decision not to attend the church nativity pageant in order to go on volunteer duty with the patrollers. Her arguing escalated until finally she shouted, "Father, you've no right to call yourself a Christian!"

Mr. Aaron glared at her angrily. "Don't you go too far!"

Mrs. Aaron tended to support their daughter. "Dear, she's right—once a year isn't too much to go to church."

Outnumbered and harassed, Mr. Aaron blew up.

"I'd hoped you wouldn't push me too far!" he barked at his daughter. "But since you do, I'm your father, and I'm outright forbidding your marrying this parson! I'm as much as any man for religion, but I won't permit my only daughter's hardhead-edness to keep her from someone able to give her a decent life."

"All right, but if I can't marry who I want to, I'll pledge my soul I'll sure never marry who *you* want!"

"One day you'll wish you had!"

"If I can't marry him"—Melissa Anne was furious—"at least I can help him tonight!"

In her fury, she bangled on the dining-table bell. The maid appeared, nervous, knowing the hotheaded Melissa Anne. "Go bring that black harmonica player up onto the porch!" Melissa Anne commanded.

When Harpin' John arrived, Melissa Anne snapped, "Go hitch up the buggy. I want you to drive me to the church!"

As Harpin' John stood aghast, she added, "I want you to stay for the afternoon rehearsal and pull the curtain between the acts as we rehearse."

Harpin' John protested. "But ma'am, I'm the only one know when to take off my barbecue when it just right done an' ready. I mean, ma'am, I just got to be there!" He needed that afternoon desperately, not only to set up the barbecue, but to oversee final details of the escape, to reduce the chances of anything going wrong.

Melissa Anne had been spoiling for a tantrum.

She shrieked, "You heard me! You're a hired darky! You do as I say!" She whirled. "Father!"

A dismayed Harpin' John read Mr. Aaron's expression which conveyed that they were both caught between a rock and a hard place.

So Harpin' John went to hitch up the buggy, his mind racing for some answer as to how he could get away . . . for there was no way he could ignore the commands of the irate white female Melissa Anne.

The nativity pageant had been in progress for almost an hour. A mile and a half away, Fletcher Randall and the planter Tom Graves were patrolling a beat around the Randall mansion veranda, smelling the combined aromas of the pots and tubfuls of the barbecued pork, beef, veal, and chicken which were being kept in readiness along with the accompaniments of cole slaw and potato salads and dozens of sweet-potato pies, plus a liberal store of liquors and beer that would guarantee an evening never to forget.

Fletcher had convinced his mother and father that he should not attend the nativity pageant in order to remain at the mansion in case some guests also might have missed the pageant and would arrive for the Christmas Eve barbecue early. And Tom Graves had joined Fletcher just to ensure that all was going well until his valued slave Harpin' John would be able to return from playing his harmonica for Melissa Anne Aaron at the church pageant.

Two horsemen came pounding up out of the night toward the mansion, and they headed directly for the clustering of lights about the veranda. The lean, slit-eyed chief patrolman Ned Smithers swung down off his horse and came striding directly to meet the advancing Fletcher.

"Bad news, Mr. Randall. It's not what you want to hear on Christmas Eve, but there appears to be a mass escape of slaves in the making. Three are reported missing from the Aaron plantation, and it seems that six are gone from your cabins—a patrolman's checking the premises now, and trying to find out from the rest of the darkies what happened."

Fletcher could imagine the means used to extract the information. He asked, "Are you absolutely certain about this?" He hoped his dismay appeared genuine.

"About as sure as I can be, yessir. I hate to make a mess out of the senator's and your big barbecue affair here, and all—" Fletcher thought that he detected a trace of sarcasm. "But the whole thing seems to have been planned to a fare-thee-well. No telling how long they've been gone." Chief patrolman Smithers paused. "And one more thing, we're looking for Mr. Tom Graves. His wife said we'd probably find him here."

Fletcher heard Tom Graves call from behind him, "Here I am. What's the problem?"

Chief patrolman Smithers turned and nodded to his assistant, who had been standing beside his horse and now came forward, holding a bundle at his side.

Smith took the bundle, which turned out to be a brown suit-coat. He held it up to Tom Graves. "Sir, can you identify this coat?"

"Of course I can," said Tom Graves. "You see my name inked inside the collar. About a year ago I gave it to my slave, the one called Harpin' John."

Fletcher felt a sinking sensation inside his stomach.

"Where is he right now?" Smithers's tone had grown harder.

"You're asking about my slave, my property," said Tom Graves, "so I'm asking why do you want to know?"

"Well, I'll tell you. This coat was found by the patrolman who discovered the slaves were missing. It'd been left behind in one of their cabins. Question is, what was it doing there?"

"Just because you came across that damned coat doesn't mean Harpin' John had anything to do with the escape." Tom Graves was appalled at the prospect of losing a very valuable piece of property, and in truth he would also miss someone as useful and amusing as Harpin' John.

"Maybe not," Smithers said. "But I have to get hold of your slave man and ask him some hard questions, and I think we'll get some truth out of him before we finish. Where can we find him?"

"He's at the church nativity pageant," Fletcher thrust himself

96

into the conversation. "I'll accompany you there. I think it would be best if I went in and brought him out. No need to cause a commotion in church. There'll be the devil to pay soon enough tonight. Once Harpin' John is in your hands, I'll go back and break the news to my father and all the rest."

The four men rode like the wind, and when they arrived at the church Fletcher dismounted first. "I'll be out as quickly as I can," he said, and went inside.

The nativity pageant had reached the point where the Three Wise Men, with young Parson Brown as their leader, were taking their leave of the manger where the Christ Child lay sleeping. Melissa Anne at the harpsichord was leading the background music with Harpin' John and two black slave fiddlers playing behind the performers, while the packed audience representing the planter families of the community murmured appreciatively.

When Fletcher Randall suddenly appeared in the church doorway, the reaction of Parson Brown and his companion Wise Men and Melissa Anne caused the audience to turn their heads. As Fletcher made his way briskly up the church aisle toward the stage, people stared incredulously. Fletcher passed by the front pews, in one of which sat Senator and Mrs. Randall. Their faces were disbelieving as their son stepped up onto the slightly raised stage, past Melissa Anne at her harpsichord, and went straight to black Harpin' John, who stood staring back at him, the harmonica still at his mouth.

"Follow me, *now!*" Fletcher said tautly, and turning abruptly he went double-timing to the door of the pastor's study at the church's right rear, with Harpin' John one step behind him. Once inside the small room, Fletcher asked quickly, "Your horse out back?"

"Yeah, what's happened?"

"No time to talk—" He snatched open the door to the steps outside. They could hear the first rumblings of the church audience. Fletcher barked, "Get your horse, I'll grab somebody else's."

Harpin' John grunted assent, asking no questions. People were starting to emerge from the church and he could hear chief patrolman Smithers shouting as the two horses pounded away into the darkness.

"Let's split up! Go to the place I showed you, I be there!" Harpin' John shouted to Fletcher, pulling his horse toward the right and lying low against its neck to avoid the dangerous low limbs of trees he raced past.

Within the forest, Fletcher's horse stepped into a groundhog's hole, and Fletcher tumbled off as the horse pitched forward, breaking its foreleg and screaming in pain. Fletcher struggled to his feet and then fell onto one knee. His ankle was badly hurt . . . he had never felt more alone.

But then, his chest heaving, he heard the distant hoot-owl sound.

Fletcher put his hands up to his mouth, and tried his best to do what he had been taught.

The hoot-owl call in response was closer.

Harpin' John checked Fletcher's ankle. "Well, we lucky, it ain't broke. But the way it already swellin', look like a real bad sprain." He looked directly into Fletcher's face. "Wasn't sure I'd ever see you no more."

Fletcher said, "I thought you were a goner, too—"

"Would of been, hadn't been for you." Harpin' John took a

long pause. "You didn't have to do what you done. How come you come in after me?"

Fletcher thought about that. "Tell you the truth, I never thought about it. I just did, that's all."

"Well, we can't rest here no longer, we got to git movin'. I know they after us, probably with dogs by now, an' we got to be either long gone or hid mighty good by daylight." Again he appraised Fletcher. "You a big man, but I can carry you to the horse, and us can both ride to a better hiding place."

Fletcher pushed himself upright again, fending away Harpin' John's help, to test himself. He tried the ankle. He winced with the pain. He managed about three hopping steps and stopped.

"It hurts. But I can make steps, especially if I lean on your shoulder. But I'd best wait just a minute—it really hurts."

"Did they all get away?" Harpin' John asked.

"I think. It sounded like it, what little I heard."

"Well, can you tell me what happened, I mean what went wrong?"

"I sure can. You gave somebody a coat, and he left it hanging in his cabin. The patrollers found it with Tom Graves's name inside, and he told them he gave it to you."

"I be damn! You mean 'ceptin' for that, we wouldn't be out here now? All we did, and that one little thing went wrong! If I could've got out'n that pageant, I really b'lieve I'd of noticed old Uncle Ben didn't wear my coat. I should've kept it when he told me he thought it was too pretty for him to wear, anyway."

Harpin' John looked at Fletcher Randall. "Well, for sure, neither one of us can't never go back. What you goin' to do? You figured out yet where you goin'?"

"I haven't had time for that. I wasn't planning on this."

Harpin' John reflected a moment. "You know, lotsa people don't realize how many white folks risks all you got, even your lives, because you don't believe slavery's right."

Fletcher thought a little while. Then he asked, "What about you? Where are you going?"

"Jes' up North, that's all I know for now." Harpin' John chuckled. "Maybe I can start me a little business cookin' good barbecue—I can do that, an' make a little music."

Fletcher determinedly pushed himself up again. He gestured that he was ready to try walking, with Harpin' John's assistance. Two hours later, deeper in the forest, they crossed a wide stream, and were confident they had eluded their pursuers.

Suddenly Harpin' John plucked from his pocket his harmonica, which he cupped against his mouth, and brought forth his patented resounding railroad locomotive *chuffing* sound.

Abruptly he stopped, whacking the harmonica against one knee. "Hey, lemme quit actin' a fool, 'cause you know what?" He stared up at the radiant North Star, joined by Fletcher. " 'Cause this here is Christmas morning now—won't be but a couple of hours 'fore the day breaks."

Again he raised the harmonica, saying to Fletcher, "Now here's a tune I don't know what it is, I jes' sort of remember it from hearin' it bein' played an' sung last Christmas when I was ridin' my horse amongst where some them new German emigrant peoples moved in the other end of Ashe County. I can't remember but jes' two sounds of the German words they was singin, they sounded something like '*Stille Nacht* . . . ' "

Harpin' John cupped his harmonica. "But I know the tune they played went like this."

He played. Fletcher heard the melody of "Silent Night" as

the Christmas moonlight bathed the faces of the black man playing and the white man listening.

When Harpin' John finished, neither man said a word. Then the pair of them resumed walking, silhouetted against the Christmas early morning sky.

Fletcher realized that now his life had changed forever, too. He thought about his parents with a sense of pain and loss that he knew both they and he would be a long time absorbing and coming to terms with. He had made an irrevocable break with his past. He knew he had made a wreck of their lives. His father's political career would become a shambles, and in Senator Randall's eyes, indeed all Southerners' eyes, Fletcher Randall would forever be a traitor. As for his mother, she'd be devastated, and he wondered agonizingly whether she would ever recover from the shame he'd brought upon her, and from the ache of losing her only child. It would be, to both of them, as if he were dead. But whatever the ache of the present and uncertainties of his future, he knew now that by not living for himself, he was learning to live with himself, at last. He'd told Harpin' John that he wasn't sure where he'd go, or what he'd do. But he remembered one thing for sure: he had some friends in Philadelphia.

About the Author

Alex Haley was born in New York and spent his early years in Henning, Tennessee. His parents were teachers, and he attended two years of college before he enlisted as a messboy in the U.S. Coast Guard, in which he served for twenty years until retiring as a Chief Journalist. He views the Coast Guard as his alma mater, since he taught himself to write during long voyages at sea. As a civilian free-lance writer, he worked for magazines, then began writing books, and his book *Roots* won the Pulitzer Prize. Haley still prefers to write at sea—now as a passenger on cargo ships—and when ashore he lives on a farm near Knoxville, Tennessee.

J $ 15.00
Haley, Alex
A Different Kind of   Christmas

       8/00